E. T Hooley

Tarragal

Or, Bush Life in Australia

E. T Hooley

Tarragal
Or, Bush Life in Australia

ISBN/EAN: 9783337056018

Printed in Europe, USA, Canada, Australia, Japan

Cover: Foto ©Andreas Hilbeck / pixelio.de

More available books at **www.hansebooks.com**

TARRAGAL'

OR

BUSH LIFE IN AUSTRALIA

2907

BY

E. T. HOOLEY

LONDON

GAY AND BIRD

22 BEDFORD STREET, COVENT GARDEN

1897

BY KIND PERMISSION I RESPECTFULLY

Dedicate

THIS LITTLE WORK TO

LORD CRAWSHAW,

OF WHATTON HOUSE, LEICESTERSHIRE,

WHO DEARLY LOVES A GOOD HUNTER WITH THE

HOUNDS IN FULL CRY, AND TO WHOM I AM

INDEBTED FOR MANY ACTS OF KINDNESS.

E. T. HOOLEY.

PREFACE.

THE following little work on Australian Bush-life was undertaken by me for the purpose of whiling away the lonely evening hours spent in a bush-hut in North-West Australia whilst engaged in forming a new sheep-station in that isolated portion of Her Majesty's dominions. I do not claim any special merit for the work; but as many of the characters and scenes are taken from life, I trust they will be found interesting to many young readers in the Northern as well as in the Southern Hemisphere.

CONTENTS.

CHAPTER						PAGE
I. OLD BEN						1
II. AN AWKWARD FIX						15
III. A MIDNIGHT MEETING						30
IV. THE BUSHRANGER						45
V. A PIG-HUNT						62
VI. WILD CATTLE						78
VII. UP A TREE						93
VIII. MURDER MOST FOUL						108
IX. THE STEEPLECHASE						123
X. HOW RACES ARE WON						139
XI. A KANGAROO HUNT						154
XII. THE ATTACK						164
XIII. TO THE RESCUE						179
XIV. THE WRECK						192
XV. GLAD TIDINGS						205
XVI. HOME AT LAST						220

TARRAGAL

CHAPTER I.

OLD BEN.

TARRAGAL, the scene of the present story, situated on the southern coast of Victoria, was in the early days of the ' fifties ' in high repute as a cattle-station. The run was originally taken up by an old Tasmanian, Ben Johnston by name, who became acquainted with an employé of those bold pioneers, the Hentys, while one of the latter's whaling-ships lay at Circular Head, on the north coast of what was then Van Diemen's Land, taking stock on board for the promised land across the water. Mr. Johnston, better known as Old Ben, worked his passage over in the stock ship, and after

I

landing took service with the Messrs. Henty for some years, thus adding to his small capital, and at length purchased a few head of cattle, and fixed upon Tarragal as his home.

Here his stock increased apace, and here in course of time he would have grown rich, but, alas for him! civilization, in the shape of a Bush inn, made its appearance on the Briar Creek, only nine miles distant, and Old Ben within two short years found that his station had passed into the hands of Angus McDonald, the innkeeper, and Ben was fain to undertake the task of droving what should have been his own fat cattle to the Melbourne market, as salaried servant. Whilst on the road, Ben was too fully occupied to find time for a spree at any of the Bush shanties passed *en route;* but his destination once reached, cattle handed over to the agent, and his cheque received, he went in for enjoyment, which meant that he never saw the sun whilst his money lasted. Two years of this life put an end to Old Ben's existence, and, like too many of his class, he filled a pauper's grave.

In the meantime, Sandy, now Mr. McDonald, had grown rich, a general store was added to his public-house, and, finding it a difficult matter to attend to a station as well, he offered the latter for sale, with six hundred head of cattle at £10 per head—stock, horses, station-plant, and runs given in—terms cash. Sandy, being a canny Scot, did not believe in bills or promissory notes.

In the course of a few weeks, a purchaser turned up in the person of a Mr. Forrester, a gentleman farmer from the English Midland counties who had emigrated to New South Wales two years before our story opens, and finding, as he thought, things overdone in the mother-colony, decided to move westward and secure a farm or station, from whence he could more easily dispose of his produce on the gold-fields, which were just then coming into notice, and where unheard-of prices were being realized—draught-horses, £100; working bullocks, £50; flour, £300 per ton, etc. Well, Mr. Forrester paid over his money, and took possession of Tarragal, settling down with his wife and three children—two daughters and one son, the eldest, Nellie, being eighteen; Katie, a wild romp, twelve; and Edwin, a fine, high-spirited boy, sixteen years. The family was accompanied by a faithful retainer, Rebecca Holt by name, who followed their fortunes from England.

Mr. Forrester soon found that he had his hands more than full, for since Old Ben's death the cattle had not had proper attention, and it took experienced hands to muster them. Again, stockyards were required, as the chock and log fences which served Old Ben's purpose to yard a few quiet cattle would not suffice now to hold some hundreds in a semi-wild state.

At this time it was simply impossible to obtain labour, as all who could find means to do so were away seeking the precious metal, and matters would have gone hard with our friends, but that Edwin and Nellie, whilst attempting to round-up a mob of cattle, were suddenly joined by two youths in stockmen's attire, who, without any saluta-tion, bore down on a magpie bullock which would persist in breaking away, and after a good rallying, in which they plied their twelve-feet stockwhips with practised skill, Mr. Magpie surrendered, and the mob were driven to the station and yarded, after which the strangers somewhat shyly introduced themselves as John and James Jackson, aged seventeen and fifteen respectively. They also stated that they were neighbours, residing only twelve miles from Tarragal, and that they were now seeking seven working bullocks which had strayed, and had probably found the Tarragal herd. Of course, they were invited to the mid-day meal, and introduced by Edwin to his parents, Mr. Forrester expressing his obligations to the strangers for their timely assistance.

During dinner the conversation turned upon the scarcity of labour, and Mrs. Forrester expressed her fears that they were doomed to pass the coming winter in two bark huts built by Old Ben, which was anything but a pleasant prospect ; upon which the elder Jackson stated that his father had an old ' Derwenter,' Jack Smith by name, who was a good Bush carpenter, and he thought it probable that Jackson *père* might spare him to Mr. Forrester for a month or two, and added that, with his father's approval, he and his brother would be glad to lend Edwin a hand to erect such of the yards as were immediately required for working the cattle.

Mr. Forrester accordingly took the opportunity of returning with the young Jacksons to their home, and upon explaining his difficulty to Mr. Jackson, that gentleman at once tendered every assistance in his power, including a bullock-team for carting timber, etc. The work was at once commenced. Stringy-bark-trees were felled by Jack Smith and Edwin, and, after being cut into nine-foot lengths, were split into slabs by the former, the brothers Jackson following with the bullock-team, and carting the slabs as well as the saplings for rafters, wall-plates, etc. A fresh site was selected for the new homestead, on a limestone plateau overlooking a small lake, which was generally covered with black swans, which suggested to Mrs. Forrester visions of countless flocks of ducks and geese in time to come.

About this time, a neighbouring tribe of natives, that had hitherto held aloof, began to make friendly advances, and were soon found useful in many ways. One young fellow, named Balgarra, in a short time became a good rider, and as an assistant stockman his services were invaluable. These aboriginals, to the surprise of the Forresters, seemed to know by instinct where to search for any particular mob of cattle. Their eyes were continually cast on the ground, which is to them what the page of a book would be to a white man.

With the assistance of friendly natives to dig post-holes and cut grass for thatching purposes, the building and stockyards made such progress that in six weeks a six-roomed cottage, built of upright slabs, with veranda in front, all neatly thatched, was habitable, only the floors being required. Here the bullock-dray was put in requisition, and a few loads of ant-hills brought from an adjacent forest, which, when well crushed and watered, made excellent floors, almost as firm as if set with cement; a kitchen was also built, in which Rebecca reigned supreme. A team of young bullocks had been broken in, and six of these, with a pair of leaders

borrowed from Mr. Jackson, were despatched to the seaport, in charge of a
teamster who came to the station seeking
employment. This man, Dick Evans by
name, was an unsuccessful digger, and his
arrival was most opportune, as the squatter
was anxious to get a supply of stores,
household effects, etc., from the port; also
Mrs. Forrester's pianoforte, the want of
which that lady felt severely, not so much
for her own amusement, although she was
a fair performer and passionately fond of
music, but that she might resume her
daughters' lessons, which had necessarily
been discontinued for several months. It
was decided, upon the return of the team, to
have a general muster of the cattle, so that
calves might be branded and the herd
counted over.

About this time, Mr. Forrester was enabled
to return, to some extent, the kindness of his
neighbour. A small run adjoining Mr. Jackson's farm was in the market, with three hundred head of cattle, which that gentleman was
most anxious to purchase, but had not the
money to put down. The difficulty was by

some means made known to Mr. Forrester, who offered to lend the sum required at a low rate of interest, which offer was gladly accepted by Mr. Jackson, and as the Red Gum —the name of the station—cattle and the Tarragal herd were often mixed, it was decided to muster the whole at the new Tarragal yards. Notice of the muster was sent to two adjoining stations, the owners of which sent stockmen to assist and bring away any bearing their station brands. The two stockmen, known as Cabbage-tree Bob and Myall Sam, were of the true Australian type of rough riders, both lithe, active young men, whose happiest moments were spent in the saddle, equipped in the strapped pants of the period, blue serge shirt, and cabbage-tree hats, with the never-failing pouch at belt, containing pipe, tobacco, and the inevitable flint and steel, wherewith to light a fire.

The evening before the muster was a busy one. All hands were fully engaged in preparations for the morrow—some making new stockwhips, others repairing old ones. The elder Jackson undertook to provide green hide hobbles for the party. Cuffs were

made from a strip of stout hide about two
inches in width, having a slit at one end
and a Turk's head neatly worked at the
other. The cuff was then slipped through a
ring in the hobble chain, and the Turk's head
through the slit, when the hobble was complete. In addition to hobbles, each rider
took a quart pot and a small supply of tea
and sugar, also some luncheon, in case they
did not find sufficient cattle before noon to
induce a return home. Mr. Forrester accompanied the party. All were in the saddle
by sunrise, each man mounted on a stock-
horse of the good old sort, now so seldom
met with, and who sniffed the keen morning air as if prepared to enjoy the day's
work.

'I think,' said Edwin, 'we had better try
the limestone ridge, in the first place. There
should be at least two hundred head between
there and the she-oak rises.'

'Well, I don't know,' replied Mr. Forrester; 'what think you, my young friend?'
appealing to John Jackson.

'I think the better plan will be to work
round by the Heathy Camp and the Kan-

ALL WERE IN THE SADDLE BY SUNRISE.

Page 10.

garoo Flat, when we can either bring what
we find there down to the ridge, and pick
up the stragglers about that quarter, or
leave the latter for another day, as they are
quiet and can be got at any time. In any
case, it will be better to work the outskirts
first; otherwise the noise and disturbance
may drive those break-o'-day boys into the
stringy-bark ranges.'

'I quite agree with you,' said Mr. Forrester.

'Yes, yes,' cried Edwin, 'so do I; you
are a trump, John, for suggesting it.'

The foregoing conversation was held as
the party proceeded on their way through
the lightly-timbered country. Balgarra suddenly turned to the right, and trotted up to
a native cherry-tree, which was covered
with ripe fruit, and commenced eating with
great gusto.

'Hullo!' cried Edwin, 'what have you got
there?'

'Budgerry this fellow, massa—plenty
yeatum black fellow.'

The tree in question was about a foot in
diameter at the base, with a short stem

which threw out numerous branches, covered with a light green foliage somewhat resembling a cyprus; the fruit when ripe is of a dark red colour, and is very peculiar, inasmuch as the stone is attached to the branch, the fruit growing from the other end of the stone. It is rather small, but most delicious.

'I say, father,' said Edwin, 'we must plant two rows of those trees in front of our new house, and make it look a little like the old home in England that you so often regret.'

'All in good time, my lad,' was the reply. 'Let us first get this cattle muster off our hands; for the present we had better keep silence, as cattle have sharp ears.'

At length the open country was reached, and a large mob of cattle descried, grazing quietly on the plain, having evidently not long left their camp. Fine bullocks that would turn the scale at a thousand pounds were there, also numerous cows in like condition, as well as a large assortment of juveniles that had not yet felt the branding-iron. The former were too fat and heavy to give much trouble, but with the latter our friends prepared to do battle.

'They appear quiet enough now,' said Mr. Forrester; 'but, in case they start off, we will work round behind that belt of ti-tree and head for home.'

Accordingly, our friends made a détour, and approached the mob on the opposite side. Suddenly a large dark red beast, with high crest and down horns, threw up his head, and no sooner had he observed the hunters than he darted away, followed by the whole mob.

'The snail-horned bull!' called James Jackson. 'Look out, Mr. Forrester; give him room, or he will capsize you. Let him go, and stop the rest.'

Now, as all were in a hand-gallop, the warning was lost upon the squatter, who, being well mounted, thought it an easy matter, for a man who in the shires was in the first flight with the hounds, to head a bull in the Australian Bush. He accordingly rode at full speed to head the runaway. Edwin followed his father to assist, whilst the stockmen, with the Jacksons, cut be-

tween the bull and his followers, turned the
mob, and succeeded in rounding them up,
which was done by ringing them in a circle
until they got winded, when they stood
facing the riders with heaving flanks and
glaring eyeballs. In the meantime matters
had not progressed so favourably with the
squatter. No sooner had he interrupted
Snailly's flight, than Mr. Bull charged the
horse, who would have given his pursuer
best ; but his rider, not being so accustomed
to wild cattle, reined him in, made a cut at
the bull with his hunting-whip, and the next
moment found himself and horse struggling
on the ground, the latter unable to rise,
owing to having got his legs foul of a grass-
tree.

ONLY JUST TIME TO SLIP BEHIND A GUM-TREE.

Page 15.

CHAPTER II.

AN AWKWARD FIX.

MR. FORRESTER immediately arose, being unhurt, and no sooner had he regained his feet than his assailant again charged him, and he had only just time to slip behind a small gum-tree, which barely covered his body, when the bull's head came with a thud against the other side. Here the furious brute kept him, as, with his head almost touching the tree, he followed round, endeavouring to transfix his foe, whose state was not to be envied, and who, no doubt, would ere long have been exhausted, had not Edwin arrived on the scene. He was close behind his father when the latter met with his fall, but, having a rather headstrong horse, he could not pull up on the spot upon seeing his father's predicament. He called

out, 'Courage, father! I'll take him off'; and
riding up behind the bull, whose whole attention was fixed on his prey, he brought his
stockwhip down with full force on the
monster's back.   This attack in the rear
took Mr. Snailly by surprise, but, nothing
daunted, he turned and charged his new
enemy, which was just what Edwin expected,
and, starting off on a steady gallop, kept
just clear of the brute's horns, and drew him
on for about a hundred yards, then suddenly put on a spurt, and soon placed several
lengths between himself and his pursuer,
upon which the latter gave up the chase
and darted away towards the ranges.   Edwin
at once returned to his father, and made
anxious inquiries as to his safety.

'All right, boy,' said Mr. Forrester; 'thanks
to Providence and to your presence of mind.
But let us see to poor Ranger, who is still
lying where he fell.'

The horse was soon extricated from his
unpleasant position, and, being unhurt, was
remounted, when father and son rejoined
their companions, and the cattle, which
were now quite manageable, were driven to

the homestead and yarded without further mishap.

Mrs. Forrester and her daughters were much interested in the account of the day's proceedings, and were loud in their praise of Edwin's courage and presence of mind. The team having returned from town well laden, the evening was spent in unpacking furniture and placing the piano in position; after which the whole party gathered around Mrs. Forrester, who played and sang for them, Nellie also playing a piece fairly well. In the Bush people manage to get a great deal of amusement in a short evening, and are generally about retiring to rest at the time townspeople are beginning their evening. Then, the former are up with the lark, and have half a day's work done whilst their town brethren are sleeping off the effects of their late hours.

On the evening in question our friends retired early, knowing that several hours' work was in store for them in the stockyard next day. Before daybreak the stockmen were moving, and had lit a good fire at the yards, where the branding-irons would be

2

heated. Edwin and his friends soon put in an appearance, laden with ropes and two long poles, with a forked end, to be used in throwing the loop over the heads or horns of such animals as they intended to catch for branding. In the first place, the mob were passed through the drafting pens, and all the strangers taken out, after which the work of branding commenced, and was quickly got through by the young men, who were nearly all experts at the work, one using the catching-rope whilst four others stood by to haul in the line, thus bringing the beast's head up to the post, when leg-ropes were made fast and the animal thrown on its side. A pole was then placed over the neck, the end of which was passed under the lower rail of the fence, a man taking his seat on the opposite end, by which means the strongest bullock can be held down. Whilst in this position the branding-iron is speedily applied, the ropes are cast off, and the operation is complete.

Work of this kind is not without danger, and men require a good deal of practice to become experts at it. But, then, a certain amount of danger adds excitement to the business. For instance, the man with the catching-pole may be in the centre of a yard in which are perhaps 200 head of cattle. He suddenly hears a whish, and has barely time to step aside to avoid being impaled upon the horns of some furious warrigal, who makes a charge on his natural foe.

In this way Balgarra had a narrow escape. After seeing Bob and Sam at work with the catching-pole, he begged hard to be allowed to try his hand, and having thrown the rope over one horn of a strawberry cow, he shouted, 'Pull away, mine catchem that fellow!' and at the same moment gave a tug on the rope, which slipped off the horn, and poor Balgarra, not finding the resistance he expected, was thrown on his back, and immediately hidden from view by a body of cattle that had come rushing round the yard, passing over him as he lay, fortunately without injuring him, as each beast in his line leaped over the prostrate form. His adventure, however, did not end here; for no sooner had he regained his legs than the cause of his disaster—the strawberry cow—having become parted from her calf in the mêlée, charged, and probably would have impaled him, had not the stockman, Bob, come to the rescue, which he accomplished by bringing the thick end of the catching-pole down with great force on the back of the animal's neck, when Strawberry measured her length in the dust, where she remained stupefied for nearly two minutes.

'Well done, Bob!' said Edwin. 'I must learn that trick; it might save a fellow's life some day.'

After this adventure the branding was continued, and before sunset eighty head had been handled, and all in the yard bearing the Tarragal brand were passed through a race and marked with hot pitch, so that they could be recognised, and *not* counted out a second time. The strangers would be kept in hand, tailed by day and yarded by night, until the muster was over, when they would be taken to their respective runs.

All fat cattle were also kept in hand, and when the muster, which lasted a fortnight, was over, the squatter found that his herd was increasing satisfactorily, and that he

could send away eighty head of prime cattle
to the Ballarat market.

Mrs. Forrester and Nellie resolved to give
the young men a treat, in the shape of a high
tea and music, on the evening of the day the
muster was concluded. Nellie spent the
afternoon in the kitchen making pastry, as
she was an adept; for, although Mrs. Forrester taught her daughters music and other
lady-like accomplishments, she determined
that they should also become conversant with
the art of housekeeping, cooking, needlework,
etc. For, said that lady, 'Of what use would
be the wife of a squatter, in these days of
scarce labour, if she could play and sing to
him of an evening, but could not cook his
dinner or sew a button on his shirt? With
the pangs of hunger unappeased, I fear he
would scarcely appreciate the music.'

It is needless to say that our young friends
spent a very enjoyable evening.

Before retiring for the night, Mr. Forrester
took Edwin aside, and thus addressed him:

'Now, my boy, I am about to place you in
a position of trust, such as, perhaps, your
years will not justify; but I have faith in

your steadiness of purpose and perseverance. Your task will be to take charge of this draft of fat cattle, and drive them to Ballarat, where you will deliver them, with a letter from me to Mr. Douglas Cameron, stock-agent. You can take Dick, the bullock-driver, and Balgarra. You must also take a pack-horse to carry your supplies and rugs. The journey will occupy about three weeks. You can make Mitchell's stockyard the first night, and the Grange the second, after which you must camp out and watch the cattle in turns. Now, what think you ? Have you sufficient confidence in yourself to undertake the task ?'

' My dear father, I am overjoyed at the thought of it. If I don't deliver those cattle safe and sound to Mr. Cameron, call me a Dutchman. I will just require a day to prepare, and Balgarra must have a rigout. Let him have a digger's red shirt, and moles to match.'

' Very well, anything in reason ; so now good-night, and be up with the lark.'

The following morning the Jacksons, with Sam and Bob, departed with their cattle, leaving Edwin and his assistant busy packing necessaries for their trip.

'Oh, Edwin,' said Katie, 'I wish I could go with you. Why was I not a boy? You have all the fun, whilst I have to stay at home poring over those dull books—crotchets and quavers all day long.'

'Never mind, little sister; I will bring you a wax doll, with real golden hair, from Ballarat. I expect they keep those necessary articles in stock down there.'

'A wax doll indeed!' with pouting lip. 'Bring me a riding-habit, and I will call you a dear, good brother. You know that Nellie's old one, which she gave me, is all in rags.'

'I fear, Katie, that the riding-habit is out of my province, so must refer you to the mater.'

Upon which Katie retired with an offended air.

The day was a busy one with Edwin. An old pack-saddle on the X principle had to be repaired—Mr. D. Altson's famous packs were then unknown—rations put away, and by night all was ready.

'Don't you think, father,' said Edwin, 'I had better get the horses shod on the Grange? I hear there is a blacksmith located there, and Hunter is getting rather tender-footed.'

'Well, my boy, do so if you find it necessary. I will give you cash for all reasonable requirements on the road.'

Edwin was up by starlight next morning, roused his assistants, Dick and Balgarra, fed the horses, and, after a hurried breakfast, started on his journey in high spirits and with a due sense of his importance as chief of the expedition. Mr. Forrester accompanied the party for six miles, until the cattle had steadied down, when, with an affectionate leave-taking, he parted with his son and returned to Tarragal. The house seemed very quiet and dull after the bustle of the previous fortnight. Edwin had never left home before, so that his mother and sisters felt his absence very much.

In the meantime, let us return to the young drover, who proceeded quietly with his cattle, and at noon reached a reedy swamp, where a halt was made for the midday meal, one watching the cattle while the

others dined.   The swamp was covered with
black ducks, four of which were shot by
Balgarra and reserved for the evening.   In
the afternoon the cattle were grazed quietly
along, and by sunset reached the stockyard,
and were safely penned up, after which the
horses were hobbled out and the camp-fire
kindled.   The ducks were then plucked and
placed on the live embers to grill, pannikins
put on the fire, tea made, and our friends
enjoyed a capital supper, the roast duck
being pronounced delicious.   The second day
out was almost a repetition of the first, but
without the ducks.   The Grange was reached,
cattle again yarded, and the blacksmith inter-
viewed, who promised to shoe Hunter early
next morning.   Whilst this was being done,
Edwin   started   Dick   and   Balgarra   with
directions to travel the cattle slowly until
he overtook them.   The evening camp was
formed on the bank of a winding water-
course, the line of which was marked by a
fringe of red gums.   Here Edwin's responsi-
bility really commenced, as the cattle had
now to be watched all night—Edwin taking
the first three hours, Dick the middle, and

Balgarra the morning watch.   One horse
was kept on tether with saddle on, so that
he could be mounted at a moment's notice,
whilst the others were hobbled out to browse
upon the rich pasture bordering the creek.
Through the first watch the cattle camped
quietly and gave no trouble. Edwin, frequently dozing, found it a hard matter to
keep awake ; he never before felt time pass
so slowly. At length the hands of the watch
pointed to eleven, and he awoke Dick with
alacrity, giving him directions in the event
of the cattle breaking away; then in a very
few minutes he was wrapped in his rug, and,
with a saddle for a pillow, was in a sound
sleep, which lasted until daybreak, when his
slumber was disturbed by a noisy laughing-
jackass, which had made his roost on an
adjacent tree.   Edwin immediately arose,
and was surprised to find that the fire had
burned low, and that Balgarra was fast asleep
beside the embers.   He next looked for the
cattle, but they had disappeared. Giving
Balgarra a shake that brought him quickly
on his legs, Edwin asked :

' Where are the cattle ?'

' Baal this fellow ! eye shuttem up little bit.'

At this moment the lowing of cattle was heard, and Edwin, quickly mounting, found the mob grazing quietly only a short distance down the brook, from whence they were soon driven back to camp, where Dick had break-fast ready. The next six days were spent by our travellers without mishap. On the plains there being abundance of grass, and in those days no wire fences to intercept their passage, the young squatter felt that he should now deliver his draft at Ballarat without difficulty and in prime condition. At length that fine sheet of water, Lake Bolac, was reached, and a halt made for the night on its northern shore.

' Mine makeum mia-mi, Massa Edwin,' said Balgarra ; ' mine thinkum big-fellow rain tumble down night-time.'

' I think you are right,' replied Edwin. ' What do you think of the weather, Dick ?'

' Well, Mister Edwin, I don't like the look of them ere clouds away to the nor'ard, over the Grampians. Unless the wind goes round, I should say we shall have a heavy shower before morning.'

Balgarra accordingly set to work to build the mia-mi, which was in the form of half an egg, with an opening to leeward. Material being scarce, he was obliged to make the frame of honeysuckle branches, which were then covered with grass, smoothly laid on and carried to an apex. Edwin and Dick laid in a stock of firewood, got supper ready, and the cattle camped by dusk. At eight o'clock the first watch was set, just as a few drops of rain began to patter on the hardened earth. Dick had the first watch, and made preparations for the storm by cutting a hole in the centre of his blanket, through which he put his head, Mexican fashion, and lighting a well-filled pipe, he was prepared to defy the elements. Edwin and Balgarra betook themselves to the mia-mi, and were soon in a sound slumber, notwithstanding that the rain was descending in torrents, covering the whole surface of the ground with water, which at last found its way into the gunyah, and under the sleepers, giving our young squatter an unpleasant shock. When fairly awake, he looked out, and could just discern Dick's form over the partly-extinguished fire.

'Well, Dick, this is a treat! The jolly water has wet all my rug. Have you been out in it all?'

'Yes, master. I have just been round the cattle. They are all right so far; but once the rain gives over, that ere Magpie bullock will canter tracks and take the lot off with him.'

'Oh, well, you had better come into the gunyah now, and I will take a turn at them. I fancy that the clouds are breaking, and that the rain will soon cease.'

This surmise proved correct, and in half an hour Jupiter made his appearance, followed by Orion and other lesser lights; but although the rain ceased, the temperature became colder, and the cattle were fetlock-deep in mud. The poor brutes, being unable to lie down, thought they would start in search of pastures new, which they accordingly did, and before Edwin, who was quickly in the saddle, could head them, they were quite a mile down the plain, in full trot, strung out in Indian file.

CHAPTER III.

A MIDNIGHT MEETING.

HEADING a mob of runaways on a dark night, and rounding them up, was anything but child's play for one rider, and it took Edwin a considerable time to effect this object. When at last he had the mob steadied, he found that he did not know the direction of his camp, and wisely thought that the best thing to be done was to keep the cattle where they were until daylight, if possible, when he would see the lake. But this intention, however well conceived, could not be carried out, as the cattle would not camp again, so he headed his charge for a bright star, Sirius, which he thought would lead him towards his companions; and after two hours' travelling began to despair of finding them, when his eyes were gladdened by the sight of a camp-fire.

'Hurrah!' he cried; 'I'm right after all.'

So he plied his stockwhip, and cooeed to his companions, hoping they would come to his assistance. His shout was answered, and immediately his cattle threw up their heads and commenced bellowing, when their cries also were replied to in kind. For a moment the young stockman was surprised, as he knew that the whole of his cattle had left camp before he did. Hearing another shout, he rode to the front, and met a horseman, who saluted him in a strange voice as follows:

'Hullo, mate, what's the row? are you lost?'

'Well, yes; my cattle broke away after the rain, and when I had got them steadied I could not find my camp, where I left two hands with the horses and traps.'

'Well, you had better come to the fire and wait for the daylight. Put your cattle to the south of my fire; mine are camped up north on a sandbank. I suppose that you, like myself, are bound for Ballarat? Whose cattle are those?'

'Yes,' said Edwin, 'I am for Ballarat. My name is Edwin Forrester. The cattle are my father's; they are from Tarragal station.'

'Oh, I know Tarragal, and have seen some good cattle on it. I once bought a small draft from Sandy McDonald, and did very well with them. My name is Clancy, and those cattle are from Mr. Bolderwood's, Eumerella run. I drive most of the cattle from that district.'

With such-like conversation, Edwin soon forgot his troubles, and when daylight appeared he breakfasted with his new acquaintance, who gave him some valuable hints upon cattle-driving, after which the party mounted.

'Now, young man,' said the drover, 'I will put you on the way to your camp. When you reach the top of that ridge, you will see the Lake Bolac, and by following its shore will have no difficulty in finding your companions, who will no doubt be on your tracks ere now. I have only one man with me, or would send a hand to help you. But stay, a lucky thought has struck me!

Why should we not box our cattle and travel together? I have only one hundred and twenty, so that the combined mob will not be too many to travel together, and it will lighten the work of watching.'

Edwin was delighted with the prospect, and expressed his thanks in adequate terms. Balgarra and Dick were picked up, and without further adventure Ballarat was reached in due course. The cattle were drafted, and Edwin took his way to the slab hut occupied by Mr. Douglas Cameron (the slab hut has now given way to a princely mansion), to which he was directed by his friend Clancy. Mr. Forrester's letter was handed to Mr. Cameron, who, after perusing it, looked with surprise at the youthful drover.

'Well, my young friend, I am glad to see you. I hope you have not had any heavy losses on the road?'

'I am happy to say not,' replied Edwin. 'I have only left one bullock, and that I sold to a shanty-keeper at the Gap for £15. He was foot-sore, and could not travel.'

3

'You did well,' was the reply; 'I will just get my horse and ride out with you to the yards, and have a look at your draft. You are fortunate in arriving to-day, as my sale comes off to-morrow morning, and there are not many cattle entered, so that we should touch high prices.'

Mr. Cameron was pleased with the appearance of the cattle, and again complimented our hero upon his successful droving in this his maiden effort, and, after showing him where to graze his charge for the afternoon, took his departure, after inviting Edwin to spend the evening with him.

The next morning Mr. Cameron was early at the yards, and busy drafting the cattle into lots of equal value—ten head in each pen. After this operation was completed, Edwin took his way to the horse-yards, where a large mob was penned, awaiting sale. They had arrived two days before from the Sydney side, and comprised some splendid animals.

Edwin was enraptured with an active-looking bay, with white feet, and small blaze down the face, standing 15.3. His

game head, set on a well-arched neck, with
his superb sloping shoulders, proclaimed
him a gentleman, whilst his round barrel,
deep back-ribs, arched loin, and drooping
quarters, were indicative of speed and
endurance. Upon inquiry from the stockman in charge, he learnt that his favourite
was highly bred, being descended from
Pyrrhus the First, with a dash of Peter Finn
blood; also that he was broken, and fairly
quiet, although he had not done much work.
Edwin walked round him again and again ;
at last, with a sigh of regret, he repaired to
the cattle-yards, where the sale was about
to commence.

A bell was now rung, and Mr. Cameron
mounted a narrow platform, extending the
whole length of the cattle-pens, and opened
the sale by reading the usual conditions.
' The highest bidder shall be the purchaser,'
etc. After keen competition, the first two
drafts of one hundred and eighty were
knocked down at good prices. Then the
first pen of Mr. Forrester's were reached.

' Now, gentlemen,' said the auctioneer,
' I have a choice lot to offer you, and from

3—2

their condition you will see that they have been carefully driven. You will find no dog-bites or whip-marks here. Now, what shall I say for this pen of prime bullocks?'

'Fifteen pounds a head!' called out a quiet little man in dealer's attire.

Sixteen, seventeen, eighteen, quickly followed, and the lot was eventually knocked down at £22 10s., after which the sale was continued with unabated vigour, and at the conclusion it was found that the Tarragal cattle made the best average of the day. An adjournment was then made to the horse-yards, when Edwin pointed out his favourite to Mr. Cameron, saying:

'I wish my father could see him; I feel sure he would buy that horse. We are rather short of stock horses, and I think he would make a good one.'

'Well,' replied Mr. Cameron, after a pause, 'I have no instructions from Mr. Forrester as to purchasing horses; but, as he entrusted you with a valuable lot of cattle, I think I may assume he has confidence in you; therefore, should the horse you fancy not go too high, I will knock him down to you.'

Edwin thanked Mr. Cameron, and took his seat on the fence to watch progress.

After several animals had been offered and sold, the bay was led out, and started at £25.

'Thirty,' cried the drover Clancy, who stood beside Edwin.

'I am sorry to find that you want that horse,' said the latter ; 'I have set my heart upon him.'

'I was not aware of that, and as I have not set my heart upon him, my lad, you may have him.'

The horse, however, had other admirers, who ran him up to £45. He was knocked down to Mr. Edwin Forrester, and our hero came forward all smiles to lead away his purchase.

The next day was spent in visiting the diggings, and watching the gold being washed out, the faces of the diggers being a study, hope alternating with disappointment, forming a capital subject for an artist's pencil.

Edwin had an interview with Mr. Cameron, who handed him an account of the sale of the cattle, with a letter for Mr. Forrester.

'I don't like trusting you with so much money, my young friend, as you might perhaps lose it *en route*, or the notorious bushranger Gardiner might relieve you of it, so I will deposit the amount with the Union Bank, and your father can draw upon that institution at convenience.'

'That will do very well, Mr. Cameron, and I cannot leave without thanking you for your kindness in buying the horse, which I propose naming Douglas, in memory of your goodness.'

'My goodness is not worth mentioning; nevertheless, I accept the compliment, and trust that you have secured a good, serviceable animal.   Should Mr. Forrester disapprove of your bargain, bring the horse down on your next trip, and I will take him off your hands.   Now fare you well, and I hope to see you ere many months with another draft of cattle.'

Taking a friendly leave of Mr. Cameron, Edwin proceeded in search of his friend the drover, as they had decided to return in company, so far as their roads lay in the same direction. No sooner had they left Ballarat behind, than Edwin, being anxious to try the paces of Douglas, proposed a canter, to which his companions agreed willingly, two of the riders keeping behind the pack-horses to see that they kept the road. Douglas went a little awkward at first, but soon settled down into the long bounding strides so pleasant to a horseman, which drew exclamations of delight from Edwin.

'It was very kind of you to let me have this horse, Mr. Clancy,' he said, 'and I hope it may be in my power to oblige you some day.'

'Don't mention it, my lad; I did not really want him, but liked the cut of his jib, so made a bid. I fancy he would make a good cross-country horse, and you know they do a bit of steeplechasing up our way.'

'Yes, so I understand; but, I say, have you heard of the last exploit of Gardiner's? I heard it talked of at Mr. Cameron's office yesterday evening.'

'Well,' replied the drover, 'I heard last night several rumours. First it was reported that he had stuck up the Bendigo Gold escort, single-handed, and shot a trooper. Then, again, that he had taken two of the mounted police that were sent out to capture him, having first shot their horses. So, you see, one does not know what to believe.'

'Very true; but a friend of Mr. Cameron's, whom I heard relate the occurrence, seemed to have the correct version, which is that two mounted troopers in search of Gardiner were encamped for the night in the Black Forest, with their horses hobbled out. Hearing the animals making off, as if startled by some animal, they picked up their bridles in haste and started in pursuit, intending to bring them back to camp.

'Well, the further they went, the further they got behind, and they came to the conclusion that their nags had broken the hobbles, and that further pursuit in the darkness would be folly, so they returned to the fire, where they had left their arms and accoutrements. As they approached the camp, lamenting their loss, they were startled by the cry,

'"Bail up there! if you move you are dead men!"

'Immediately there stepped from behind an iron-bark-tree the figure of a man, rather above middle height, with bushy whiskers, clad in mole pants, monkey jacket, and cabbage-tree hat. In his right hand was a Colt's revolver, and in his left three pairs of handcuffs, which he had just taken from the troopers' saddles.

'"Now, my friends," said the stranger coolly, "I will introduce myself. My name is Gardiner, and I dare say you have been very anxious to make my acquaintance; and now that we have met, I have no doubt that we shall part good friends— that is, if you obey orders. But if you cut up rusty or make the least attempt to escape, by the Lord Harry I will let daylight through your carcases!"

'The unfortunate troopers were in a trap, and felt powerless, so they were fain to promise obedience.

'"Here, then," said the bushranger,

throwing the handcuffs, "slip a pair of those bracelets on each of your wrists."

'When this had been done he cast down another pair, saying,

'"Now, then, one of these cuffs on the right hand of one and left hand of the other. That is well. Now you may start for Ballarat, and give my compliments to your chief. Tell him that he will hear of me at Bendigo to-morrow."

'As the unfortunate men were starting away, he called them back, saying:

'"I see you had not finished supper when I interrupted your meal, so you may drink your tea and take this piece of damper. I will take care of your rations and fire-arms for the Government. You are not likely to require them again."

'The poor victims then tramped back to their barracks, coupled together, feeling thankful that the darkness of night enabled them to reach home without attracting attention. Rather a sharp trick of the bushranger, was it not?'

'H'm! sharp enough, in truth; but I wish I had known as much before leaving Ballarat. I knew Master Gardiner (that is not his real name) when he was horse-breaking in our district, and feel sure that he has thrown the police off the scent by stating that he intended to go to Bendigo. I should not be at all surprised if he has gone westward, where he knows every inch of the country. If so, we may have the bad luck to fall in with him, and that for me would be a serious matter, inasmuch as I have £300 of my savings in this valise, which I intend to invest in land at the sale on the 25th, and it would be hard lines to part with it to a rascally highwayman. I would rather risk a shot from his revolver and have a gallop for it, although I fear old Grampus would not stand much chance, as Gardiner is always well mounted.'

'I'll tell you how we can circumvent the rascal in the event of an encounter,' said Edwin. 'Let me carry your valise, and, as I am a light weight, I will give him a run with Douglas—I believe the horse is fast; moreover, the bushranger would not imagine that a boy would be entrusted with the valuables of the party, and most likely would not think it worth while to pursue me.'

'It is a happy thought and well conceived, my young friend, but I could not think of allowing you to run the risk. In the first place, he would be certain to send a shot after you, which might prove fatal; in which case I should never forgive myself.'

'I have no fear of that, and don't agree with you about the shooting. He would simply think that the boy had galloped off in a fright. You may depend upon it he would keep his eye on you as the most dangerous, as well as the most profitable, mark; therefore, dismiss your scruples, and give me the valise.'

CHAPTER IV.

THE BUSHRANGER.

'WELL, really,' said the drover, 'the plan is so good that I cannot refuse to take advantage of your generous offer ; so here is the valise, and good luck attend you.'

During the foregoing conversation our travellers were making good progress; and, as the day proved warmer than usual, a long halt was made at the fighting waterholes. The horses were hobbled out, billies boiled, tea made, and an enjoyable lunch discussed ; then, as old Sol began his descent to the westward, our friends resumed their journey, keeping a good look-out and moving in Indian file through all narrow passes. At night, whilst around the camp-fire after the evening meal, pipes were lit, and our travellers began to laugh at their fears, and considered now that all danger of meeting the bushranger had passed.

'I am inclined to think,' said the drover, 'he really intended going to Bendigo, after all, as he told the troopers. You see, they would not believe him, and would come to the same conclusion that I did at first—that he meant following a different course. There is now very little danger of being robbed, although there are often a lot of roughs about Burnbank public-house. However, we will not stop there, so there will be nothing to fear.'

Our friends arose early, refreshed with a night's slumber such as can only be enjoyed by camping in the open air in mild weather; and by sunrise they again started on their way merrily, Clancy calculating his chances of obtaining the coveted piece of land at the upset price, and Edwin guessing what they were doing at Tarragal. Balgarra amused himself by humming a native chant, in which 'whitefellow budgerry' played a prominent part, when suddenly, from behind a granite boulder, a horseman appeared within ten paces of the travellers.

THE BUSHRANGER WAS MOUNTED ON A COAL-BLACK HORSE.

Page 47.

It needed not the salutation of 'Bail up there! No d——n nonsense, or I will drop one of you!' to tell our friends who was before them. Bushy whiskers, mole pants, monkey jacket, and cabbage-tree hat, were all there; not forgetting the revolver in his right hand, levelled unpleasantly close, Edwin thought. The bushranger was mounted on a coal-black horse, very nearly thoroughbred —a grand animal, but rather low in condition. It needed but a glance to show that he was superior to the common run of hacks. In an instant the thought flashed through Clancy's brain, 'It's all up with my £300.' At the same time he replied to the summons to 'bail up' by inquiring, 'Who are you that interrupt peaceable travellers?' and moved his horse as if to pass on.

The revolver was at once levelled at his head, and again the bushranger called out:

'Halt! If you move a yard you are a dead man; but only behave sensibly, and give up your money, when you may ride on your way.'

'I have no *money*,' Clancy would have

added, but he was interrupted by an excla-
mation from the highwayman, and, on looking round, he saw that Edwin had started
back on his tracks at a gallop.

The bushranger suddenly threw up his
arm, and immediately the crack of his revolver resounded through the still morning
air. Edwin's hat fell to the ground, but he
rode on, apparently unhurt. Gardiner, with
an oath, again raised his pistol, and was
taking a deliberate aim, when the drover
caused his horse to swerve and cannon
against the other's steed, so the second
bullet whistled through the air over-
head.

‘ D——n your eyes, you shall pay for that !’
was the response. ‘ I’ll have that young
whelp also. I shouldn't wonder if he has
the plunder, and I’ll make sure of finding you
when I come back ;’ saying which, he turned
his revolver upon Clancy’s horse, fired, and
poor old Grampus rolled over in the dust,
shot through the shoulder-blade, and after a
few spasmodic kicks expired. The drover
was rather shaken by his fall, but struggled
to his feet and raised the faithful old steed’s

head on his knee, and, with tears in his eye, wiped away the life-blood that oozed from the fatal wound.

But we must now leave the sorrowing drover with his dead steed to follow our hero and the bushranger. No sooner had the latter seen the result of his shot, than he started at full speed in pursuit of Edwin, who was now nearly 200 yards in advance, with Douglas well in hand. Looking back, he was surprised, and, to say the truth, dismayed, to find that he was pursued by so terrible a foe. He now began to realize that an encounter with a bushranger was rather a serious matter, and that it bore a somewhat different aspect this morning to what it did by the camp-fire overnight. However, possessing a stout heart, he resolved that he would not give in without a struggle, so, sitting down in the saddle, he shook up his horse, and found Douglas respond cheerfully to his call.

A clear stretch of open country now lay before the horsemen, who were heading to the eastward, both steeds having settled down to their strides, and the bushranger

4

was surprised to find that he did not gain more rapidly upon the chase. Edwin had now reason to be thankful that while in New South Wales he had resided within sight of the Homebush Racecourse, where his chief amusement was to rise early and trot his pony down to the training-grounds, there to watch the racers undergo their training. Here on several occasions he rode a gallop for a friend of Mr. Forrester's, who wanted a light-weight for a trial. Being naturally a sharp lad, he took notice of the jockeys, how they rode, with hands well down on the withers, elbows close to the side, knees perfectly still, and toes slightly inclined outwards. After a few trials, Edwin found that he could imitate those riders fairly well.

On the present occasion, believing that his life was at stake, he strained every nerve to keep the lead, hoping that his pursuer would tire of the chase; but he soon found that that hope was in vain: not only was the bushranger still in pursuit, but, from a hasty glance thrown over his shoulder, Edwin believed that he was gaining upon him, therefore he wisely eased his horse for a short distance, taking a steady pull at him. And so mile after mile the chase continued, until at length Douglas's want of condition began to tell, and it was evident to Edwin that his fine horse was almost run out. A belt of she-oaks now appeared on the left, and towards those Edwin now shaped his course, leaving the road which he had hitherto followed, but soon repented his act, for he found himself crossing one of those treacherous crab-hole flats which are so prevalent on these plains. Here the uneven ground caused Douglas to labour more than ever, and twice he nearly fell.

'Stop, you young dog, or I'll fire!' was shouted close behind him, and Edwin, in despair, resolved to resign himself to his fate; he cast a glance over his shoulder before finally doing so, when, to his surprise and delight, he saw the bushranger and his horse rolling over on the plain, the horse having put his foot into a crab-hole, which, owing to the pace at which they were going, caused him to throw a somersault, landing his rider some yards in advance. The black horse was quickly on its legs, and trotted up to Edwin, who had pulled up at some 200 yards' distance, and who could scarcely yet realize that he was safe. The prostrate bushranger still remained where he fell, and Edwin began to think he was killed; so, after catching the black horse, he dismounted and slackened his girths as well as those of his captive. Douglas was much distressed and covered with foam, but the wiry black, being more accustomed to the work, was in much better trim.

'I don't like to leave that poor wretch there without some assistance; he may be dying,' soliloquized Edwin, looking in the direction of his fallen foe; 'but, on the other hand, he may be only foxing, as a trap for me.'

Whilst thus communing with himself, the object of his thoughts resumed a sitting position, felt his head in a dazed sort of way, and after a few moments got on his feet, but found that he could not stand, having sprained an ankle badly. Again lying on the ground, he caught sight of Edwin, and called out:

'Come and lend me a hand, young fellow; I am badly hurt. You need not fear; I'll not harm you now. Just help me on my horse, and you may go scot-free.'

'Thank you for nothing,' was the reply; 'I am quite free as it is, which is perhaps more than could be said should I get within range of your revolver. If you are badly hurt, stay where you are, and I will give information at the sheep-station about five miles beyond where you stopped us, and they will no doubt send out for you. The Government reward will be worth the trouble.'

So saying, he mounted Douglas, and, leading the black, started off in the direction of his companions, followed by a volley of oaths and threats from his fallen foe. With what different feelings he retraced his steps now that all danger was passed, as, with a light heart, he cantered gaily along! Nevertheless, he was anxious to know how it fared with his friend Clancy, and also to relieve the anxiety which he knew would be experienced as to his fate. Upon rounding the turn before mentioned, he was delighted to see his companions in safety, standing around the dead horse.

'Why, what is the matter with Grampus?' were his first words.

'Thank Heaven you are safe!' shouted the drover, starting forward and wringing our hero's hand. 'What has become of Gardiner? and how came you in possession of his horse? I feared that he would have served you as he did poor old Grampus, whom he shot in cold blood before starting in pursuit of you; but I am dying to hear your story.'

'Well,' said Edwin, 'there is not much to tell.' Whereupon he related all that had occurred in his absence, adding: 'Now, as the rascal deprived you of your horse, you had better take possession of his.'

'I will do so for the present,' said the drover; 'but of course the authorities will claim and advertise him, for there is little doubt that he has been stolen from his rightful owner.'

Clancy quickly changed saddles, putting his own on the black, and stowing that of the bushranger on the pack-horse. Then, taking a sorrowful leave of old Grampus, our friends resumed their westward journey, the encounter and chase of the morning forming the chief topic of conversation.

'You had better take care of the valise yourself now,' said Edwin; 'you are quite as well mounted as I am, and I have not so much confidence in my ability to save your money as I had yesterday. Indeed, had it not been for that fortunate crab-hole, the rascal would now have been in possession of your savings, and I should have been tied to a tree, and perhaps left to starve. But we had better not think of that. Let us turn off to the sheep-station, now visible in that valley, and we will give information which may lead to the capture of our late antagonist.'

'I fear that is not likely,' replied Clancy. 'You may depend upon it he would scramble away somehow, and would ere long get assistance—for, bad as he is, you would be surprised at the amount of sympathy he gets from a certain class. However, we will report what has taken place, and then wash our hands of the business.'

Upon reaching the station, they were informed that Mr. Hamilton, the proprietor, was at home, and would see the travellers. He was soon made acquainted with the adventures of the morning, and seemed somewhat incredulous, until Clancy pointed out the bushranger's horse.

'Your story certainly has surprised me,' said Mr. Hamilton; 'but come into my office, and I will take down your statement. I am a justice of the peace, so we will proceed in proper form.'

When the statement had been taken down and signed by the drover and Edwin, Mr. Hamilton said:

'Now, my friends, we will have some dinner; and by that time my horses will be driven in from the paddock, when I will despatch a spring cart to bring in the vagabond, should he be seriously hurt; or should he have made off, and we should be able to capture him, what say you to assisting? You would share the reward, which is, as you are doubtless aware, £1,000.'

'I would rather not be mixed up in the business,' replied the drover; 'and I think my young friend here is anxious to get home. So, with your permission, we will push on.'

'Well, just as you please,' said Mr. Hamilton; 'but I insist upon your taking some refreshment. Your men will find accommodation at the hut, whilst you two must dine with me. I am a bachelor, and am always glad of a guest or two. If you leave your address, I will let you know the result of my Gardiner hunt by mail next week.'

Taking a friendly leave of Mr. Hamilton, our friends again turned their horses' heads westward, and travelled thirty-four miles without a halt, then camped for the night at what they considered a safe distance from their crippled foe. Five days later Edwin, having parted from the drover, reached Tarragal, where all were delighted to see him, and his sisters most eager to have an account of his adventures.

'I see you have a fresh horse,' said Mr. Forrester. 'Where did you get him ?'

'I bought him, father, hoping that you would approve of my action. But read Mr. Cameron's letter, and after tea I will relate

my adventures in full, and I can promise you
they will be rather interesting.'

Mr. Forrester, having read his agent's
letter, was in ecstasies at the result of his
cattle sale, and very pleased at the compliments paid to his son's droving.

'Well, my boy, you have acquitted yourself with credit, and I trust that, with God's
blessing, you will continue as you have begun.
With respect to your purchase, I can't say
that I altogether approve of giving too high
a price for a stock horse; but you deserve
something out of your successful under-
taking, so I will make you a present of the
horse, and hope you will take good care of
him.'

'No fear of that, sir, as you will acknow-
ledge when you hear that I owe, perhaps,
my life, and most certainly my liberty, to his
speed and endurance.'

'Why, what do you mean?' said the
squatter. 'Have you been in danger of
losing one or the other?'

'I have indeed; but, as the danger is past,
and I am terribly hungry, we will postpone
the recital until after tea. At present I am

most anxious to discuss the mater's currant luncheons and tea-cakes.'

Mrs. Forrester, whose maternal anxiety was aroused, had tea sent in without delay; and after partaking thereof, the whole party, including Rebecca, drew around Edwin, who recounted his adventures from the time of leaving Tarragal until his return. His account of the meeting and chase by the bushranger drew tears from the eyes of his mother and sisters.

'Oh,' cried Katie, 'what a dreadful man! Do you think he would have killed you?'

'Of course, I cannot say what he might have done. I hear that he is not blood-thirsty as a rule; but there is no doubt he was savage with me for leading him such a chase.'

'What can the police be about?' said Mr. Forrester. 'They should have captured that scoundrel months ago. Why, in England he would not run a week!'

'Well, you see, father, he is not in England; and I think I have heard of the London police being months on the track of robbers without running them to earth.

Besides, see what advantage a smart bushman has, who knows the country, over new-
chum police, who have, perhaps, lived in
town all their lives, and who would not
know a wombat from an opossum! Nothing
like experience. Witness your overthrow
by the snail-horned bull. Had you been an
old bushman, father, you would have given
him room to pass on.'

'Don't crow too soon, young man! You
will have to do some more cattle-hunting
ere long, and I may have a laugh at your
expense.'

'But,' said Mrs. Forrester, 'do you think
Mr. Hamilton would find the bushranger
where you left him? It is a pity that your
friend Clancy did not go back and assist in
the capture. Of course, *you* were quite right
to keep out of danger.'

'That is reasoned like the dear mother
you really are; but do you think I would
have permitted my companions to undertake
any risk without sharing it with them?'

'Quite right, my boy,' said his father.
'Never show the white feather or do a mean
action if you wish to keep a clear conscience.

From what I have heard of Clancy, it was not fear that kept him from accompanying Mr. Hamilton's party.'

'True,' said Edwin. 'He told me that, being on the road so much, and meeting all sorts of people, he deemed it politic to keep clear of entanglements of all kinds, as he never knew when he might want assistance during his travels. Still, I am sure he would be pleased to hear of Gardiner's arrest, more particularly as he feels very much the loss of his favourite horse. By the mail due on Saturday, I should hear from Mr. Hamilton.'

CHAPTER V.

A PIG-HUNT.

Upon the arrival of the mail, the following letter was handed to Edwin :

> ' Mount Pleasant,
> ' *March* 7, 18—.

' Dear Sir,

'Shortly after you left I proceeded with two white men and a black tracker, all well armed, to the spot where you last saw the bushranger. We had no difficulty in running the horse-tracks from the road to where the chase ended. We saw where the black horse fell, and from thence tracked the robber into a clump of she-oaks, where we lost all trace of him.

'I believe he is still in the neighbourhood, and shall not be surprised to hear of some station having been struck up by him at any moment.   I have forwarded your statement to the Chief Secretary.

'Trusting that you reached home without further mishap,

'Believe me,

'Yours very truly,

'W. HAMILTON.'

'MR. EDWIN FORRESTER,
    'Tarragal.'

'Well, it seems the rascal has escaped, after all,' said Mr. Forrester, after perusing the letter. 'I only trust he will keep clear of our district, and that he will meet his deserts ere long.'

'Oh, Edwin, you have not heard of our new neighbours,' said Nellie. 'A gentleman named Murray, with his family, have come to reside at Briar Creek, and have taken a lease of Baylup Farm. Mr. Murray is a doctor, and stipendiary magistrate as well. They are such nice people. Mrs. Murray is so kind and lady-like, and her daughter, Ida, is such a dear girl. I called upon them with papa and mamma, and they will return our call in a day or two; so you must be at

home to meet them.   I am sure you will
like Ida ; she is just about your age, and so
very jolly.'

'Oh, bother ! I am not going to make a
fuss over a lot of girls.   I suppose you will
want to get up riding-parties, and will expect
me to be on duty for the occasion ?   Ride
the hacks with a long skirt, etc.   But, I tell
you candidly, I shall not have time for that
kind of nonsense.   Now, if Mr. Murray had
a son or two, that would be jolly.'

'If you had given me time to finish my
story, I should have told you that Ida has a
brother—a young gentleman about nineteen,
I should think.'

'Well, now, I call that rich ; why could
you not have told me about this young fellow
at first ?   What is he like ? And what is his
name ?'

'I can scarcely tell you what he is like,'
replied Nellie ; 'but you will see for yourself shortly.   His sister adores him, and calls
him Carmel.'

'I hope he can ride, as we mean to have
a wild-cattle-hunt shortly, and I will ask him
to join us.   What do you say to a ride this

afternoon? I want to let you see how Douglas goes.'

'Just the thing; I have not been in the saddle since you left. You might take Katie also. She has been wishing for a ride.'

'Very well; let her know, and get ready whilst I get the horses saddled.'

In a few minutes our friends were in the saddle, Katie radiant with the prospect of a gallop.

'Let us go down to Irishtown,' she cried, 'and see the men digging potatoes.'

Irishtown was so named from a few sons of Erin having recently settled on some rich flats, with the object of growing potatoes, at that time a very profitable industry.

The riders were cantering briskly along through a patch of wattles, where only a Bush track had been cleared, and upon rounding a turn almost collided with a horseman coming at a canter in the opposite direction.

The latter's horse suddenly shied, and threw him at the feet of Edwin and Katie, who had some difficulty in preventing their horses from trampling upon the fallen man. The stranger was soon on his feet, and, in answer to our hero's inquiries, replied that he was not much hurt, and, raising his hat, thanked Nellie for having caught his horse, which had come to a standstill beside her, after throwing its rider.

The stranger was a young man of about twenty summers, of medium height, with a remarkable Wellington nose, and a clean-shaven chin, contrasting strongly with the bushy whiskers so common in those days.

'Can you inform me how far I am from Tarragal?' said the stranger, addressing Edwin. 'I am bound for that station, and anxious to arrive before night.'

'You will easily do that,' was the reply. 'I am just from Tarragal, which is four miles from here. The place belongs to my father.'

'Oh, then I am glad to have met you. I am the bearer of a letter from a friend in Sydney to Mr. Forrester, whom I am anxious to see. My name is Yardly Mildman, and my father is a clergyman of the Church of England. He thinks of coming to live in this neighbourhood.'

'Let me introduce my sisters,' said Edwin. 'And, as we are out only for pleasure, we will return and lead you to your destination.'

Upon arrival at the homestead, the young man presented his letter, which proved to be from a Sydney friend of Mr. Forrester's, introducing the visitor to his notice in the usual terms.

Mr. Forrester received the stranger most cordially, and introduced him to his wife, who at once invited him to spend a few days with the family. During the evening Katie set herself to the task of quizzing the stranger, who did not seem to be a very brilliant young man.

He informed Mr. Forrester that his father, who was still in Sydney, had been written to by the Bishop of Melbourne, offering him the appointment of chaplain of the Briar Creek district. Before, however, accepting the post, he decided to send his son over to report upon the prospects of the new district. In reply to Mr. Forrester, he stated that his family had only arrived from England a few months before, and that, as might be guessed from his ignominious introduction, he was not an experienced horseman.

'That difficulty will soon disappear in Australia,' said the squatter. 'If you are here next week you may see and assist at a cattle-hunt. We have some scrubbers that I mean to shoot for beef.'

'Nothing would please me better,' was the reply, 'so long as I have a quiet horse and the country is pretty clear; but I fear that I shall not be of much assistance to you, but will do my best.'

The afternoon following the arrival of young Mildman brought Mr. and Mrs. Murray, with their son and daughter. After the usual introduction had taken place, the young people adjourned to the veranda, whilst the elders discussed afternoon tea. Mr. Murray was a fine specimen of an English gentleman, and one who, in the dual capacity of doctor and magistrate, inspired confidence and respect. His wife was gentle in manner and lady-like in demeanour, and quite won the heart of Mrs. Forrester by her praises of the poultry-yard.

Edwin was delighted with Carmel, who

promised to join in the cattle-hunt. Ida also, he was obliged to admit, was not so bad as she might be. Yardly Mildman was introduced to the latter, but did not seem to make much impression. With Edwin, however, she chatted gaily, and was invited to inspect Douglas, who was greatly admired by both the young lady and her brother.

'You young people might organize a riding-party for to-morrow afternoon,' said the squatter. ' Take a run over to the Creek and show Mildman what our district is like. The population is not yet very large, but is rapidly increasing. By the way, I saw Mike Nolan yesterday. He was in great trouble, owing to the wild pigs having got into his potato patch and committed much havoc amongst the mealies.'

'I should like very much to have a ride over to the Creek,' said young Mildman, ' if your son can spare time.'

'Well, that is agreed,' replied Edwin ; ' and perhaps you and your sister will join us. We can go round by Baylup and pick you up.'

'Thank you. I am sure it will give us

much pleasure to join you, but I hope you
will drop the " Mr." when addressing me.
My name is Carmel, and, if you don't mind,
I shall call you Edwin. I dare say we shall
soon know each other well enough to dis-
pense with formalities.'

' Agreed, with all my heart ; and now
come and have a look at our lake. We
must get a boat, when we can invite our
friends for a sail.'

The lake was duly admired, as were the
black swans gliding so majestically on the
still water. Here the young people lingered
until a *cooee* recalled them to the house,
where Mr. and Mrs. Murray were ready to
depart, having promised to renew their visit
ere long.

Shortly after lunch the next day, Edwin,
with his sisters and their visitor, started for
Baylup, the latter being mounted upon one
of the quiet old stock horses. A little over
an hour brought the riders to their destination, where they found Ida and her brother
ready equipped.

' What do you say to a turn up the Black-
boy Valley ?' said Carmel. ' We can come

round by Irishtown afterwards, and see the potato-diggers.'

This proposal was agreed to *nem. con.*, and the young friends started gaily, after being cautioned by Mrs. Murray against reckless riding.

'I will put Ida under your care, Miss Forrester; she is rather inclined to be a reckless rider, and Fleetwing is very spirited —she does not get half enough work.'

'Oh, mamma, you are unjust to dear Fleetwing! She is a pet, and I am sure she would not hurt me for the world.'

'Very well, dear; I hope your confidence will not be abused. Come back early; our young friends must have tea with us before returning to Tarragal.'

The Black-boy Valley was a charming spot, rich grassy slopes leading down to a running spring of beautiful fresh water, a number of grass-trees, with their tall straight stems and graceful, drooping, palm-like tops, adding to the picturesqueness of the scene.

'What a pretty spot!' cried the girls in a breath.

'But what a pity to plough the grass up in that way !' exclaimed young Mildman.

'That is where the wild-pigs have been rooting,' said Edwin; 'I wish we had brought a gun: we might have had a shot. There must be a lot close around; those tracks are quite fresh.'

'What fun to have a pig-hunt!' cried Katie. 'Let us catch a small one, Edwin, and take it home. You can wrap it in my saddle-cloth; it is half a blanket, you know.'

'Is it not dangerous sport?' inquired the stranger. 'I have read of pig-sticking in India, where horses are often killed by wild-boars.'

'Very true,' replied Carmel; 'but there are not many very large boars out here, although young Nolan told me yesterday that one turned upon him in the potato-field and nearly gored his horse, after which he set a kangaroo dog upon it; but the poor brute soon came to grief, having been ripped open by the boar's tusk.'

'I should give that gentleman a wide berth in case of meeting him,' said Mildman.

'I suppose it would be impossible to kill him without a gun ?'

'Not at all,' replied Edwin. 'I heard Cabbage-tree Bob say that he could knock down and cripple any pig with a blow from a small stick across the loins ; it creates concussion of the spine, and paralyzes the animal, after which he is powerless.'

'There they are !' shouted Carmel ; ' see, just beyond those ferns.'

And away the whole party started in pursuit.

There were nine pigs of various sizes, one old warrior bringing up the rear.

'Look out !' cried Carmel ; 'that must be the brute young Nolan told me of—don't get too near him !'

The young Englishman, however, had now entered into the spirit of the chase, and, having a good steady mount, thought to show the young ladies that he was not quite a muff on horseback. Accordingly, he headed the boar three several times, and tried to stop him. The monster, however, only gnashed his teeth, and continued his course. Mildman, not to be balked, and unheeding the warning shouts of his companions, again charged, this time at closer quarters, when the brute suddenly made a leap at the horse's neck, causing the animal to swerve, and the saddle, which had not been very firmly girthed, slipped round and deposited the unlucky horseman almost on the pig's quarters.

A shout of dismay rang out from his companions as they saw him fall, expecting to see the monster turn his attention to his fallen foe, who remained for some seconds where he fell, expecting every moment to be his last. However, to the great relief of all, the boar was seen in full pursuit of the riderless horse, making frantic leaps at the latter's throat. No sooner was the boar at a safe distance than the discomfited hunter leapt to his feet, and scrambled up an adjacent banksia-tree, and it was not until he had reached a distance of ten feet from the ground that he realized he was safe.

His companions now gathered round— with the exception of Edwin, who had ridden off after the stock horse—and congratulated Mildman upon his lucky escape. A shout from Edwin soon drew attention in his direction, when he was seen tying the runaway horse to a branch, after which he galloped away, and shortly was seen circling round towards the clump of ferns, waving his hat. His companions soon joined him, after seeing the fallen man remounted, when they found Edwin in chase of the boar, who was now pretty well exhausted, his high living on new potatoes not being conducive to speed and endurance.

'We will run this fellow to a standstill directly,' he cried; 'he is too fat to keep it up much longer in this heat.'

In a very short time the boar came to a stand, and stuck his head in the branches of a fallen tree, where he remained panting and exhausted.

'Now for a stick,' cried Carmel; 'who is anxious to try Cabbage-tree Bob's method with the stick? No fear of missing his back; it is a broad one.'

'Hold my horse, somebody,' said Mildman. 'I'll have a crack at him; where shall I get a stick?'

' There's a fine stringy-bark pole over to your left,' he was told; so, dismounting, he picked up the pole, a dry one, about seven feet long, and three inches in diameter at the thick end.

Walking cautiously behind the pig until within reach, he quickly drew aside and brought his pole down with terrific force over the boar's back, expecting to see the monster fall prone to the earth. To his dismay, however, the pole, which proved to be rotten, broke into three pieces, and before the broken ends had reached the ground Mildman was in full cry for the nearest gum-tree, up which he shinned with amazing dexterity. The boar, which he imagined to be in full pursuit, did not even grunt his disapproval of the assault, of which he seemed quite oblivious, and it was soon apparent that his long run had proved too much for him, and that for the present, at least, he was helpless. However, no one felt inclined to try the knocking-down process again. Accordingly, the friends bade adieu to Mr. Pig, proceeded on their way, and in due time reached Baylup, where the account of their adventures drew roars of laughter from Mr. Murray.

'I should think you are becoming rapidly colonized,' was that gentleman's remark to young Mildman. 'A few such experiences, and you can write a book of your travels.'

CHAPTER VI.

WILD CATTLE.

Two years have passed away since the events recorded in the last chapter. Briar Creek has now become Briar Town; the rich arable lands bordering the Creek have been bought up by agriculturists, and improvements effected at a rapid rate. Our old friend, Sandy McDonald, is rapidly growing rich, and is the largest landed proprietor in the neighbourhood. A church, school, court-house, and police-station have been added to the town, also a new hotel, and on an adjacent slope stands a pretty little parsonage, occupied by the Rev. George Mildman, who, upon the recommendation of his son, had accepted the living. About this time a public meeting was held in the long room of the new hotel, when it was resolved to hold a race meeting on St. Patrick's Day. Messrs. Forrester, Murray, and Jackson were elected stewards, and a subscription-list started which filled fairly well.

Tarragal, also, had progressed with the times. A new stone house had been erected to replace the slab building, which had been burnt down on black Thursday. A nice garden, stocked with fruit-trees, surrounded the house, and the homestead gave the impression of comfort and prosperity.

Mr. and Mrs. Forrester were much the same as when we last saw them, but the young people had shot up as they can only do in this genial climate. Nellie was a full-grown young lady, of gentle and refined manner, whilst Katie talked of long dresses, and wondered whether she would be permitted to go to the race ball. Edwin was now a sturdy young fellow, with the down of manhood making its appearance on his chin. He had become his father's right-hand man, and knew every beast on the station, was a fearless rider, and would send Douglas at full speed through the thickest forest, where

fallen trees often proved no mean obstacles. He was a general favourite in the district, and the idol of his mother and sisters.

The young people were often together, and it soon became evident that Carmel Murray was deeply attached to Nellie, who, however, received his attentions with an apparent indifference that often cast a cloud over his good-natured features. It was also remarked that our friend Edwin did not persist in his objections to riding-parties. On the contrary, he was most eager to get up short expeditions for a day's duck-shooting, a kangaroo-hunt, knap or cherry picking, etc., on which occasions our hero generally contrived to ride with the fair-haired, blue-eyed Ida, who was now an accomplished horse-woman, and managed her steed, a high-spirited descendant of the renowned Norval, to perfection.

On returning from one of those impromptu outings, Edwin and Ida found themselves in the rear of the party of equestrians, who were leisurely wending their way homewards, enjoying the delicious south-westerly breeze, which in this neighbourhood blows delight-

fully cool throughout the summer. The gentlemen had had a good day's sport with their guns ; the spoil, in the shape of several black ducks, was suspended from the saddle D's, whilst our old acquaintance, Balgarra, carried a black swan, swung over his shoulder.

'I hear, Edwin,' said Ida, 'that you intend running Douglas for the steeplechase on St. Patrick's Day. Is it true ?'

'Yes, Miss Murray. I shall give him a spin ; he fences very well, and has a pretty good turn of speed, so should have a chance, although I shall ride him a few pounds overweight.'

'Do you intend riding him yourself ? 'I do hope you will win, if only for the credit of our district. But what says Mrs. Forrester ? Is she not afraid you will get hurt ? I have seen her very anxious when you have been out after cattle a few hours later than usual.'

'Well, I have had some trouble with dear old mater about the race, and, indeed, she is not yet reconciled to the idea ; but, after all, it is not so dangerous as chasing wild cattle

in the stringy-bark forest. The races will
not come off for two months, so I trust
that long before that time arrives I shall
have the consent of all parties and I hope
you will wear my colours on the eventful
day.'

'Oh, I shall be most happy to do so, as,
I am sure, will all our party. Dear old
Douglas is a great favourite with us all.
Carmel is most anxious to get a horse or
two for the races; he means to be in the
steeplechase if possible, but in any case I
think he will run Dauntless for the Maiden
Plate; Carmel says he is very fast for a
mile. I think I must run Fleetwing for
something, if papa will permit; she can go
like the wind with my weight. I ran a large
emu down last week on Biscuit Flat, in
about three minutes.'

'I think it would be a pity to race Fleetwing; nothing spoils a lady's hack so quickly
as racing; you see, whenever you start for
a canter in company, a horse which has
been trained thinks he is in a race, therefore
wants to gallop, which is not always pleasant
for a lady; besides, Fleetwing is very high-

spirited as it is, and must try your wrists pretty well at times.'

'She is rather troublesome occasionally,' replied Ida; 'but she is very good tempered, although excitable, and I can manage her without difficulty.'

'Come along, you two sluggards!' shouted Carmel. 'Let us have a canter, or we shall be late for tea.'

So saying, they all cantered off, and before the sun had quite disappeared Tarragal hove in sight, and in a very short time they had gathered round Mrs. Forrester's hospitable board, and recounted their shooting exploits.

'What about our next wild-cattle hunt?' inquired Yardly Mildman, who was one of the party; 'the last one was great fun, and I have a better horse now, so expect to enjoy it.'

'I think of getting ready for it on Monday,' replied Edwin; 'and will start Dick Evans out with the bullock-team and supplies, with orders to camp at Spring Creek. We can then ride out on Tuesday afternoon, and commence operations on Wednesday. To-morrow I will send Balgarra over to let the

6—2

Jacksons know about it. We have had two good yards erected, with long wings, so that with a fair run of luck we should make a good haul out of the Warrigals. I mean to carry a light carbine, in case we fall in with the Snailly bull. If so, I shall give him a broadside or two.'

'A good idea,' replied Carmel; 'the brute wants shooting. Did you hear about the McKays falling in with him a short time since on the Moleside, and firing at him?'

'Yes,' said Edwin; 'I met George shortly afterwards. He told me that they fired seventy-five rounds at him from a pepper-box revolver, and then, having expended their ammunition, had to leave him.'

'Ha! ha!' laughed Carmel, 'that is a good joke. But what could they expect with a weapon like that? The only wonder is that they did not shoot each other.'

'Well, I don't think it will take seventy-five shots from my carbine to bring him down; but I must not boast too soon, or he may overthrow me as he did the governor.'

Mrs. Forrester having persuaded her guests to remain all night, an impromptu dance was arranged, and the evening spent as pleasantly as could be desired.

On Monday morning Dick was despatched with the bullock-team, with orders to camp at Spring Creek, where he should await the coming of the hunters. Upon the arrival of the latter next day, Dick was found to have formed camp, pitched the tents, and had baked a damper.

'Well, Dick,' said our hero, 'did the bullocks camp well last night?'

'Why, I got no sleep at all, Master Edwin; they were on the move all the blessed night. They are clumpers, they are, I tell you. Why, that there Noble will stop close at hand a-ringing of that there bell, while his mates get about a mile away, and then he will start off at full trot after them. All the while I'm thinking, d'ye see, that they are all right, because I can hear the bell. Only that I had the old horse, they would a' been at Tarragal before morning.'

'You should hobble Noble, Dick; that would stop his trotting proclivities. It will not do to lose the bullocks, as we may want them all in a day or two.'

Further conversation was interrupted by the arrival of the Jacksons. Horses were hobbled out, and pannikins put on to boil, and our friends drew around the fire to enjoy the good things provided by Mrs. Forrester and Nellie.

The company now consisted of the brothers Jackson, Carmel Murray, Yardly Mildman, Edwin, and Balgarra, who were to do the stock-hunting, Dick's work being to mind camp and look after Noble and Co. The site of the camp was well chosen, being a beautiful grassy plat of rich black soil, through which trickled a rivulet, that took its rise in the ranges about two miles distant. The winding course of the stream was outlined by banks, fringed with ti-tree and sassafras, whilst the back country was timbered with eucalyptus and giant stringy-barks, as yet untouched by the woodman's axe. After passing through this flat the stream is lost to sight, having disappeared in the loamy soil, where, no doubt, it finds its way to the Southern Ocean by some of those subterranean pas-

sages for which this limestone country is so
famous.

After regaling themselves and smoking
the pipe of peace, the hunters pulled some
long grass, and spread their rugs, and, with
saddles for pillows, turned in for the night.

Before the first streak of day had appeared,
Edwin was up, and, after lighting the fire,
called out:

'Now, then, roll up, you fellows; we must
be in the saddle as soon as it is light, or those
Warrigals will be off to their den.'

His companions quickly responded to the
call, and in a very short space breakfast was
despatched and horses saddled, each rider
being provided with a coil of raw-hide rope,
with an iron ring at the end, the use of which
will be described in due course. A short rope
with a noose was also tied around each
horse's neck. Stockwhips were dispensed
with, as on the present occasion they would
be a useless incumbrance. Edwin also carried
his carbine. After proceeding half a mile, the
elder Jackson inquired:

'Which way shall we steer? I think there
should be a mob on the open heath.'

'Most likely,' replied Edwin; 'but let us
first go up to Old Ben's look-out, from
whence we can get a good view of the
country.'

Accordingly, a course was shaped for a
round, grassy hill, lightly timbered with she-
oaks. No sooner had they reached the
summit than exclamations of delight broke
from the hunters; for there in full view on
the plain, only a mile distant, appeared a
large mob of cattle of various sizes, from
full-grown bullocks to calves only a few
weeks old. After gazing at the quarry for a
few moments, the horsemen descended the
hill.

'Now,' said Edwin, 'we must make a
détour to the right, so as to cut them off
from the forest. It will not do to get to
windward; they are as keen of scent as a
deer. When they start, I will take the right
wing, with Balgarra to follow. You, John,
take the left, with your brother. Carmel and
Yardly will tail up. We must run them for
the Kincairn stockyard, which is on the edge
of the forest, with a long wing extending to
the south. Keep them together, if possible;

but if they break, use the ropes, for we must not go home empty-handed.'

So saying, a start was made in the direction indicated, the hunters moving silently along. At last a cough from one of the horses gave the alarm, and the cattle were off on the instant, all heading for the line of timber, only three-quarters of a mile distant.

The horsemen now took their allotted places, each feeling within him a spirit of emulation, which urged him to do his utmost towards bringing the chase to a successful issue.

For a quarter of a mile the mob kept huddled close together, amidst a cloud of dust; but beyond that the most determined forced their way to the front, and it was soon observed that their old enemy, Snailhorn, led the van, with tail extended, and the foam of anger flying from his nostrils.

'Now, then, old man,' cried our hero, 'here's at you!'

So saying, he ranged alongside, and gave him a shot from the carbine, firing from the hip. He directed the shot at the left shoulder, but at the moment of firing the bull made a sudden swerve and charged his horse, which caused the rider to miss his aim, the bullet only grazing the withers. After this failure Edwin reined up, and allowed the bull to get into his stride again, when, with a sudden rush, he darted alongside, fired, and had the satisfaction of seeing the bull turn over on his back, after which he writhed on the ground, the life-blood spouting from his nostrils.

'Hurrah!' shouted our hero. 'Snailly has run his last race.'

Then, casting down his carbine, he put his horse to top speed, and was soon in his place on the wing. The cattle were, so far, heading in the right direction.

After a mile had been traversed, the heavy-weights began to get winded, and commenced to drop off one by one, and if interfered with, at once charged, so that no time was lost with those stragglers, the riders following the main mob. At last the timber covering the wing of the yard was reached, and, not-withstanding the efforts of the horsemen, about twenty head broke away.

'Never mind that lot,' shouted Edwin;

'close upon the others. Keep at them, and they must run into the yard.'

And in less than a minute a mob of fifty-five were inside and the rails up. A very mixed lot to look upon, several bearing the Tarragal brand, but the majority were clear skins, amongst which were some grand-looking cubs.

'Now for the others!' cried Edwin. 'Come along, boys; let us have some fun.'

And amidst the wildest excitement the six riders started in pursuit of the cattle, which broke away at the wing, each man uncoiling his rope as he galloped along.

'I mean to have that roan cow,' called Carmel; 'she is a beauty.'

'Look out for her horns,' shouted John Jackson. 'I know her of old; she's a tartar at close quarters.'

'Here goes for the brindle bull!' cried our hero, swinging the noose of his rope clear.

Each then rode up to his beast, and, keeping behind until he found a fair chance, suddenly darted up alongside, and threw the noose over the animal's horns or head, as the case might be; then, holding on to the other end, carried it along until a tree was reached, when the rider passed to the opposite side to that taken by the beast, and, hauling on the rope, quickly made it fast with two half-hitches, and then as speedily as possible put himself and horse beyond the radius of the rope.

After securing the roan cow in this manner, Carmel essayed to get beyond reach of her horns; but the cow was too quick for him, and gave his horse a severe gash on the haunch. Four head were in this way secured by the white hunters. Yardly Mildman did not attempt this difficult feat, and Balgarra, when last seen, was in chase of a cub away to the right, heading for a clump of ti-trees. Several cattle were still in view, making for the forest at their best pace.

CHAPTER VII.

UP A TREE.

'COME along, Jim,' cried John Jackson, 'let us have that spotted cow; she is one of our lot.'

Away the five riders again started in pursuit, the Jacksons singling out the cow, a full-grown animal in prime condition. The elder brother seized hold of her tail whilst still at a gallop, and swung himself from the saddle, letting his horse go loose; and as the cow turned to charge him, he, with a peculiar jerk, threw her on her side and, passing the tail between the hind-legs, held her down without difficulty by hanging on to the end of the caudal appendage. James Jackson in the meantime had dismounted, and, with two leg-ropes taken from the necks of their horses, secured fore and hind feet.

'Well,' said Carmel, 'I call that a good morning's work, and vote we now go back to camp. I feel rather peckish after my gallop.'

'Yes,' replied Edwin; 'we will get back to camp, and bring Dick out with the bullocks, and couple our prisoners to them. But what about Balgarra? When I saw him last he was in full chase, so most likely has secured something, although he has not had much practice with the ropes.'

'I saw him closing up with a bull cub,' replied James Jackson, 'and I should think he might manage that fellow. He was just entering that belt of scrub at the time.'

A move was made in the direction indicated, and the tracks easily picked up, and after following the trail for a short distance a *cooee* was heard, which was easily recognised as Balgarra's. The call was immediately answered.

'Come on,' said Edwin, starting at a gallop; 'perhaps he may be in want of assistance.'

Beyond the belt of ti-tree was an open flat, upon reaching which the riders sud-

BALGARRA WAS PERCHED UPON THE TOP OF A GRASS-TREE.

Page 95.

denly reined up, and a burst of hearty
laughter rang out, whilst the scene that met
their gaze certainly justified such a proceeding. Poor Balgarra was perched upon
the top of a grass-tree, scarcely five feet in
height, in the centre of the flat. The cub,
a fierce young brute about eighteen months
old, was standing at the foot of the tree,
making frantic passes at the black fellow's
legs, which were kept continually on the move
to avoid the brute's horns—the said horns
being encircled with the noose of the raw-
hide rope, the loose end of which was trailing
on the ground. Balgarra's horse, an old
stager, was quietly grazing about a hundred
yards away, quite unconcerned at his rider's
danger. Seeing the horsemen halt, Balgarra
called out :

'Come on, Massa Edwin ; catchem tail.
Him berry near killem mine to-morrow
morning. Him turnem over mine yarraman,
then me jump up here !'

'Well,' said our hero, laughing, 'you
seem very comfortable up there, so might
as well remain while we go back to the
camp for Dick and the bullocks; the bull

can't hurt you very much, you know, and we will bring you some dinner when we return.'

'What for you borack makeum? Mine can't stop here dinner-time; me directly tumble down dead fellow. This bull sulky fellow too much.'

'Oh, very well, we will get you out of your fix. What say you, Carmel, to try your hand at a throw? Do you think you can manage that fellow?'

'Oh, I think so,' was the reply; 'at all events, I will try. But what about getting up to him? I should not like to get Dauntless crippled; he is badly hurt already.'

'No danger of that,' said Edwin. 'I will ride close by, and draw him away from the old stump; then, when he is in pursuit of me, you must rush on to him.'

The plan was at once put in operation, and in a very short space the cub was seized and thrown by Carmel, and secured by his companions, Balgarra taking his revenge by bestowing sundry kicks on the prostrate bull.

All hands now started for the camp,

where a treat was in store for them in the shape of a kangaroo steamer, Dick having shot a 'boomer' close by. After luncheon the bullocks were taken to the scene of the morning's operations, James Jackson and Balgarra being sent to the limestone ridge for a mob of quiet cattle, which were intended to steady the wild ones now in the yard.

Upon reaching their captives of the ropes, no time was lost by the hunters in coupling each one to a working bullock, the latter, with their prisoners, being then left to find their way to Tarragal at their leisure, and on the second day they were all found safely at the home paddock-gate, when they were driven to the stockyard and liberated.

But we must return to Spring Creek. Upon the arrival of the quiet mob, they were driven to the stockyard and mixed with the wild herd, when a general fight ensued, and an amazing quantity of sand was thrown up by way of challenge. After they had somewhat settled down, the hunters mounted, returned to camp, and prepared to pass another night. While seated round the fire, the day's battles were fought over again, and Balgarra had to submit to a large amount of chaff on the subject of his encounter of the morning. Yardly Mildman's adventures of long ago were again recounted for the edification of the Jacksons. Mildman, who was not at all a bad fellow, joined in the laugh against himself, and vowed that his next pig-hunt should have a different termination.

Early next morning our friends were *en route* for the Kincairn stockyard, and took their places between the wings, prepared to receive and steady the mob. When all was ready, the rails were let down, and the cattle came out with a rush, but were stopped at once, and rounded up; and after a few minutes a start was made, the two Jacksons riding in front to prevent a breakaway, the four others keeping close order on the wings and tail. All went well with the expedition, and by nightfall the whole mob was safe inside the Tarragal yards, and the hunters received many compliments upon their success.

Edwin's first inquiries were for Douglas,

who was now supposed to be in training.
So wending his way to the stable—

' Well, Joe '—to the tiny groom who did
duty in the improvised loose-box—' how is
the old horse ?'

' He is in fine spirits, sir, but he's a brute
to pull. I started him for a canter this
morning, as you told me, down the flat;
but he soon got into a gallop, and I had to
run him at the horse-paddock fence to stop
him. I thought he meant jumping it, and
I believe he would, too, only I hung on to
the off-rein with both hands.'

' I am sorry you had to do that, Joe, as
it may teach him to balk; but never mind,
I will give him a little schooling in the
morning.'

The promised schooling was got over
before breakfast next morning, after which
some hours were spent in the stockyard
branding, etc. The scrubbers—as they were
called—were then turned into a safe paddock, where they would be kept until sold
as store cattle.

' I think,' said Carmel, 'we should look up
those men at work on the race-course. Sup-

pose, Edwin, you return with me to-morrow to Baylup, and we will ride over the course together?'

'Agreed,' replied the latter; 'I want to take Douglas in to have his shoes removed. I have a colt also that should be ridden, so will take Balgarra as well.'

Another musical evening was spent at Tarragal, and Carmel was in the seventh heaven, as he found Nellie more gracious than usual; in fact, the young lady in question was not blind to the fact that Carmel was deeply in love with her, but was wise enough to refrain from giving him any encouragement until she had analyzed her own feelings. However, on this occasion she allowed the ice to thaw to some extent. She had always liked Carmel—who was a great favourite with the whole family—and began to think that to love him as he deserved would not be a very dreadful calamity. Yardly Mildman was also an ardent admirer of Nellie's, and the two often sang duets, much to the annoyance of Carmel, who was not at all musical.

During the evening it was decided that

Nellie should accompany her brother to Briar Town on the morrow, for the purpose of procuring sundry articles requisite for the ball dresses, now in course of preparation.

In the morning an enjoyable ride of two hours brought our friends to Briar Town, where they were warmly received by Mrs. Murray, who was alone, Ida having accompanied her father, who had driven a few miles out of town to see a patient. They were expected back about noon.

Edwin saw the smith, and had Douglas shod, when he returned to Baylup, and found Mr. Murray at home, who, after a hearty shake of the hand, left him with an apology, as he had to transact some magisterial business for Chief-Constable Bloater, who had been awaiting his return.

'Well, Bloater, what can I do for you? I hope you have no more of those shearers locked up. The poor fellows get punishment enough in the loss of their money, and from the effects of bad liquor.'

'No, sir; the town was pretty quiet last night; but I wanted to know what I am to do with those Chinamen. One hundred and thirty of them passed yesterday from South Australia, where they landed to evade the poll-tax. They are bound for the gold-fields.'

' Well, have they paid the poll-tax? Have you seen their passes? Are they all in order?'

' Yes, sir; the passes seem quite in order, but there are so many of them. They might take it into their heads to kill some-one.'

'Nonsense, Bloater! Why should they molest anyone? I am sure all those that I have seen are peaceable enough, and only intent upon getting eastward as quickly as possible to their friends on the diggings.'

' Oh, well, sir, you know best; but I don't like the pig-tailed beggars, and never shall. They crowded into McDonald's store in dozens, crying out " Chow! chow!" which I have no doubt means that they would chaw him up. ·He sent for me, as he was afraid of them, and could not get rid of them; but as I was busy writing a report for the Inspector, I could not go down just then. I heard afterwards that the bullock-driver who is carting their luggage got McDonald to sell him five bags of rice, so that, when I went with my men, all well armed, they seemed quiet enough, and were all busy cooking.'

'No doubt,' said Mr. Murray; 'and, had you been a little later, you would most probably have found them busily *chawing* the rice, which I am sure they would find more palatable than old Sandy's carcase. However, you may send one of your men out on their trail, if you like, just to see what they are about; and, by the way, Bloater, you had better ask the Inspector to send up a few extra police for the races on Easter Monday, as there may be some roughs about.'

'Very good, sir; I will, sir. Good-day, sir.'

'That man,' said Mr. Murray, entering the house, 'claims to have been in the British army, but I don't think he is of the sort that won Waterloo!'

'Well, Edwin,' addressing our hero, 'how did you leave your father and Mrs. Forrester? It is nearly time that they came over to give me my revenge at whist.'

'All at home are well, sir, and I am sure my father is as anxious for a rubber as yourself. Carmel and I intend riding over to inspect the race-course this afternoon. Will you accompany us? I would like to have your opinion about that short turn leading into the straight.'

'Well, I think I may promise that,' was the reply. 'And, Ida, you may as well come with us; Fleetwing wants exercise, she will be getting unmanageable directly.'

Edwin was gratified at learning that Ida was to be of the party, which was exactly what he hoped for, but dared not say so.

'You know I am always glad of a canter, papa,' said Ida; 'but when you are so much engaged, and Carmel away, there is no one to ride with.'

'Oh, as to that, you might press young Mildman into the service occasionally; I know he is fond of riding, and his mother was regretting yesterday that he did not get more of it.'

Our hero did not quite approve of this turn in the conversation, and felt rather relieved when dinner was announced, it being customary at Briar Town to take the principal meal at one o'clock. After dinner the party visited the race-course, and found the improvements in a most advanced state. Edwin put Douglas over two of the steeple-chase fences in good style.

'He seems to like the work,' said Mr. Murray. 'If he is fast enough, I think you have a good chance of winning the steeple-chase, Edwin.'

'How beautifully he jumps!' cried Ida, delighted. 'I am sure he will win. He is a noble animal.'

'He does fairly well,' replied Edwin, 'but wants a great deal more practice at the business. I will come down in the morning and give him once round over the six fences; those two he cleared just now are only four feet two inches, the others are two inches higher. The stewards talked of sending us over that lane by the burnt bridge, where the road of the new bridge branches off, but gave up the idea on account of the roadside drains, which would most likely throw a horse when he landed.'

'It is a dangerous place,' said Mr. Murray, 'and I objected to it from the first. In fact, that old road should be stopped up by a fence; a traveller on a dark night might ride on to the old bridge and get killed. I must see about it.'

The evening was spent at Baylup, with music and dancing, Yardly Mildman and two of his sisters making up the party. Before retiring for the night, Carmel and Edwin arranged to go down to the course at day-break and exercise their horses, the former having put Dauntless in training, notwith-standing a slight lameness, the result of the roan cow's horn.

The gallops were performed satisfactorily, and the six fences safely negotiated by Douglas without a hitch, after which the friends started upon their return to Baylup, where breakfast would be awaiting them. Upon passing an old road leading from the creek towards the course, Edwin's attention was attracted by a fresh footprint crossing the said road, and he paused a moment to examine the track, saying to his companion:

' What can have brought anyone out here so early this morning on foot ?'

' Oh, it must be some of those loafers about Sandy's,' was the reply. 'Perhaps it was some unlucky beggar who had not money enough to pay for a bed, so camped out.'

'Come along, or we shall be late for breakfast.'

Accordingly, our friends proceeded on their way. Upon nearing the township, it was quite evident that something unusual had occurred, as knots of people were congregated in the streets, talking eagerly, and all very much excited.

CHAPTER VIII.

MURDER MOST FOUL.

'WHAT can be the matter?' said Carmel; 'I trust there is nothing wrong at our place.'

'Come along,' cried Edwin, turning pale, and, putting Douglas at a hand-gallop, he was soon amongst the crowd making inquiries.

'What is the matter? Has any accident happened?'

'Yes, Master Forrester,' replied a sturdy bullock-driver, 'something has happened; but I don't know as how you would call it an accident—much worse than that. Mr. McDonald was murdered last night in his bed.'

'Good heavens!' cried out both young men; 'how dreadful! Is there any clue to the murderer?'

'Oh, I see Mr. Bloater down there, and he says he can put his hand on the right man in no time!'

'Come along,' said Carmel, 'and let us see my father; I have no doubt he will have all particulars from the police.'

Upon reaching Baylup, Mr. Murray was found on the veranda in consultation with the Chief-Constable, who appeared stupefied with the dreadful occurrence.

'Can you get no clue to the perpetrators of this dreadful crime,' inquired the magistrate, 'or as to the motive of the murder? Was any robbery committed?'

'I don't think the villains took anything, sir—leastways, any money; for the safe is securely locked, and there is nothing in the shop till.'

'Well, I hope you have instructed your men to keep the people away until you have a chance of picking up the tracks? I will come down immediately after breakfast, and call a jury together for the inquest.'

'Well, I don't know about the tracks, your worship. We have not a good tracker in town, and I can't see the use of bothering about the tracks, for there have been so many people in to see the body, that the road in front of the building is like a sheep-walk.'

'Oh dear! oh dear!' exclaimed the magistrate. 'Why did you not keep the crowd away? It was a great oversight on your part. See that you remedy the mistake as far as possible. Lock up the room until I come down.'

'This is a dreadful thing, sir!' said Edwin, as the constable departed. 'If you have no objection, I will go down with Balgarra, who is an excellent tracker, and assist the police.'

'Do so, by all means, and I am sure Bloater will be very glad of your assistance. But come in; let us first have some breakfast, and then to work.'

Soon afterwards, Edwin and Carmel walked down to the police-station, taking Balgarra.

'Mr. Bloater,' said the former, 'we have come to offer our services in assisting you in this dreadful business. My boy, Balgarra, is a capital tracker, and I shall be glad to accompany him myself, and try whether we can pick up some clue to this horrid crime.'

'I don't see the use of tracking,' was the reply, ' and don't want any interference with the police. The police are quite able to settle this business. We will have the murderer before long, never fear.'

'I am very glad to hear it,' said our hero. ' My offer was made with the best of intentions. I would also like to draw your attention to a fresh track, which I saw this morning when returning from the race-course. It appeared to me strange that a man on foot should have been out there so early in the morning. Would you not like to see it ?'

'Tut, tut ! no ; I don't want to see it. Why, if I went to see every track reported to me this morning, I should be run off my legs.'

'Oh, very well,' said Edwin, somewhat offended to find his offer treated with such contempt. ' I have nothing more to say, and will wash my hands of the business.'

By this time Mr. Murray had arrived, and the inquiry was held in the long room of the hotel. It transpired that the deceased closed his house at eleven, and retired to a detached building, which he used as a bedroom and office, where it appeared that he did some writing before going to rest. It was presumed that he locked and bolted his doors and windows in accordance with his usual custom, so that his assailant was probably concealed in the room beforehand. There appeared to have been no struggle; one blow with a tomahawk on the temple did the business. Robbery did not seem to be the object, for the safe-key was found in the dead man's pocket, and his watch under the pillow. After a careful inquiry, the coroner summed up, and the jury returned a verdict of wilful murder against some person or persons unknown.

Edwin informed Mr. Murray of the result of his interview with the Chief-Constable, and the magistrate was very much annoyed thereby.

'The man is an idiot,' said he. 'He is not competent to cope with a case of this kind. I must write to the Superintendent on the subject, and have a detective up.'

Our friends now returned to Mrs. Murray's, and things in Briar Town again resumed their usual course, notwithstanding that the founder of the town lay still uncoffined.

The Traveller's Rest was closed for the time being, and the key taken by the police, pending further instructions.

The family at Baylup were still discussing the tragedy, when Mr. Murray was informed that the Chief-Constable wished to see him.

'Well, Bloater, what is it?'

'Why, sir, I think of applying for warrants for those Chinamen who passed the other day; I feel sure they are the murderers.'

'Have you reason to suspect any of them of the crime, for of course they could not all have been concerned in it, and you surely do not mean to arrest over one hundred men on suspicion?'

'Well, not the lot, sir; but I might round them up, pick out a few of the most suspicious characters, and run them in.'

'Really, Bloater, if it were not such a serious matter, I should be inclined to laugh at your folly. As it is, I am astounded. Pray, say no more about it.'

8

'Very well, sir; but you might let me have a few blank warrants signed, so that I may be able to arrest any suspicious-looking characters that I may fall in with. I could then bring them before your worship for a hearing.'

'Why, Bloater, this sad business seems to have scattered the little wit you ever possessed to the four winds of heaven! Do you suppose that I am so void of common-sense as to sign warrants for you to fill up at will? Take my advice: go home and have a sleep, after which I hope you may be able to collect your senses.'

So saying, Mr. Murray withdrew and left him.

'I am not at all satisfied about the track we saw this morning,' said Edwin; 'I think I will take Balgarra and run it up a bit.'

'Do so, by all means,' was the reply; 'and Carmel can accompany you.'

'Why not leave the matter in the hands of the police, papa?' said Ida. 'Suppose Carmel and his friend came upon the murderer: he might kill them. It is too dreadful to think of!'

'Well, I think those two young fellows, backed up by Balgarra, should be able to cope with one man,' said her father. 'So banish your fears, and give us some dinner, so that they may set to work. In the meantime, I will write a note to Mr. Forrester, asking him to ride over and assist me with his advice.'

As Mr. Murray left the room, our hero found himself alone with Ida, who turned to him, saying :

'I do hope you will be careful, and not incur any risk. You know I shall be so anxious about Carmel.'

'I would like to think that you were a little anxious about me also, Miss Murray.'

'Of course I shall be,' was the reply. 'I am always anxious when I have friends in danger.'

At this moment Nellie entered the room, and the conversation turned to other topics.

After dinner, the friends mounted and proceeded to the spot where the suspicious track was seen. Balgarra had no difficulty in picking it up. The man had been walking

rapidly, and rather erratically, not keeping
a direct course or picking the best travelling
ground. After a time, a patch of soft loam
was crossed, where the track was clearly
defined. Here Balgarra halted and dismounted for a closer inspection. After a
few seconds he arose, and, turning to Edwin,
said :

'Gipsy George this way walk, morning
time little bit. Too much cranky fellow.
Nothing straight walk.'

Gipsy George was a splitter of timber,
well known in the district, a hard-working
man who spent months in the forest while
fulfilling a contract, but no sooner did he receive his money than he would make a bee-
line for the Traveller's Rest, and, handing
his cheque over to the landlord, would know
no more until told that he must clear out, as
his money was done. He would then betake
himself to the stringy-bark ranges for another
term, when the scene would be re-enacted.
He had been noticed by Carmel a few days
previously at the Traveller's Rest, shouting
for all hands ; therefore the young men came
to the conclusion that he had now taken to

the Bush in a fit of delirium tremens, which belief was supported by his uncertain rate of progression.

The tracks were followed until night, by which time the trackers had travelled a long distance ; but, owing to the circuitous route pursued, they were only five miles from Baylup, towards which they now turned their steps, with the intention of spending the night at home, and returning at daybreak to the tracks.

Mr. Murray was much concerned by the young men's report, and urged them to lose no time in following up the tracks next day. Rations were got ready overnight, and hobbles strapped on to the saddles, as Edwin expressed his intention of finding the man before he returned again. If not quickly discovered, he was in danger of perishing for want of water.

Our young friends were in the saddle before daybreak, and were soon on the spot where the track was left the previous evening. Balgarra again took the lead, and, keeping his horse at a sharp walk, followed the trail over stony rises and through stringy-bark flats without a halt. At eleven he pulled up and shouted to his white companions, who were quickly at his side.

'This way get down Gipsy George. Me thinkum little bit sleep. Pickaninny axe throw away.'

And, dismounting, he picked up a toma-hawk, which he handed to Edwin.

The latter, upon taking the implement in his hand, cried out :

'Good heavens, Carmel! Look at this! The tomahawk is covered with blood!'

A light seemed to break upon the minds of both young men. It was now evident that they were on the track of the murderer, and doubts arose as to whether the deed was committed whilst the perpetrator was in possession of his senses. They were now more than ever anxious to overtake the runaway. Balgarra was accordingly directed to pursue the trail, which he did, with his companions in close attend-ance.

About noon, when Edwin had some thoughts of casting about for a water-hole, where they might make a short halt, he saw the black boy suddenly rein up and make a signal for silence. Then, turning to his companions, he said in a low voice :

' Me hearum white fellow yabber-yabber.'

After a few moments' attention, the friends heard what appeared to be an excitable conversation, the sounds coming from a thickly-timbered gully. Upon approaching the spot, a most pitiable sight met their gaze, for there, in the fork of a fallen gum-tree, appeared Gipsy George, perfectly nude, with the mid-day sun sending its fierce rays full upon his unprotected head. In his hands he held a long pole, with which he made frantic passes at an imaginary foe. Directly he caught sight of the horsemen, he rushed towards them, crying out :

' Save me ! save me ! they are after me in hundreds !' And with a yell he darted between the horsemen.

The young men dismounted, and approached the unfortunate man, and after a time contrived to allay his fears, when they gave him a drink of water from a leathern bottle, which the poor wretch was sadly in need of. Carmel had some difficulty in tearing the bottle from his lips. Balgarra hunted about, and found the fugitive's clothes, after which he was put on the pack-horse, which Balgarra led. A détour was made to a water-hole, and some tea made, when the captive was induced to take a little food. His cry was 'Water! water!'—the great thirst created by the fiery liquor being unquenchable.

Night had set in before the party reached Briar Town. Carmel had ridden in advance to consult with his father as to what should be done with the unfortunate man, also to acquaint him with the conclusions arrived at by himself and Edwin, drawn from the blood-stained tomahawk.

'This is important news indeed,' said the magistrate; 'but say nothing about it to anyone just now. I will send down for a constable, and have your prisoner taken to the lock-up, where he can have proper treatment. To-morrow I will examine him in my medical capacity.'

Upon the arrival of Edwin and his captive, the latter was handed over to the constable, who had instructions from Mr. Murray for treatment of the prisoner.

Our young friends put up their horses, and had a plunge in the creek, after which they found their way to the parlour, where Mrs. Murray and her party were awaiting their presence for tea.

'Well, boys, I hear you have found that unlucky man, Gipsy George, and have been the means of saving his life?' said Mrs. Murray, after first greeting her son and his friend.

'Yes,' replied Carmel, 'he certainly would have perished had we not fallen in with him.'

Then a warning glance from his father informed him that the ladies were not acquainted with the sanguinary part of the story.

'Papa is in town, Edwin,' said Nellie, 'and purposes taking me home to-morrow. Shall you return with us?'

'Yes, by all means,' was the reply. 'I have been neglecting my work sadly of late, and Douglas is being neglected, too.'

'Your father will be here shortly,' said

Mrs. Murray. 'He had to attend one of those tiresome Roads Board meetings, so could not come to tea.'

'Now you young people must adjourn to the drawing-room and have some music. Ida has been so intent on this ball that I fear her practice suffers.'

A move was made to the drawing-room, the elder lady remaining to give directions to her domestics.

'Now, you noble cavaliers,' said Ida, 'give an account of yourselves. It appears that, after all, you encountered only poor old Gipsy George, who will undoubtedly kill himself some day with his intemperate habits. But what is the matter? You both seem as serious as the proverbial judge!'

CHAPTER IX.

THE STEEPLECHASE.

'WELL, Sis,' said Carmel, 'if you had been in the saddle from before daybreak until night, you would be as serious and tired as we are; so we must ask you and Miss Forrester to show your Christian forbearance, eschew curiosity, and give us some music.'

'So we will, dear boy. Come, Nellie, let us cheer these dull boys up a little.'

At which they went to the piano, and, selecting some pretty duets, played until Mr. Murray came in, accompanied by Mr. Forrester.

'This is a serious business,' said the latter to his son. 'I have heard of your own and Carmel's discovery from Mr. Murray. You will both have to give evidence at the ex-

amination as soon as the poor fellow recovers
his reason.'

The young men's fatigue was a sufficient
reason for early retirement; and next morning Mr. Forrester, with his son and daughter,
started homewards. On passing through the
township, the Chief-Constable called Edwin
aside, saying:

'I have been thinking that perhaps I had
better have a look at that fresh track you
told me of the other day. Would you mind
showing me the spot?'

'I fear it would be little use to show you
the spot now,' replied Edwin. 'Why, the
track is over two days old, and, as the town
herd travel in and out every day over that
ground, all traces must be obliterated ere
now.'

So saying, he rode away, and left Mr.
Bloater to pursue his discoveries as best he
could.

A week later Mr. Forrester, who was a
justice of the peace, was requested to attend the police-court, for the purpose of
giving Gipsy George a hearing. Edwin also
had notice to attend at the trial. The toma-

hawk found by Balgarra was identified by several witnesses as one kept by the inn-keeper in his warehouse for opening pack-ages, and which was missed on the day of the murder. The blood - stains were ex-amined by Mr. Murray under a powerful magnifier, and pronounced human.

The culprit, who seemed now quite re-covered, could give no satisfactory account as to how the weapon came into his posses-sion. Several witnesses saw the prisoner late in the evening, previous to the murder, at the Traveller's Rest, in an inebriated state ; and one witness had heard him using threats and abusing the landlord, who refused to supply him with more liquor.

After hearing the evidence, the magistrates committed the prisoner to take his trial on the capital charge at the next general sessions, to be held in Melbourne, where I may say that a verdict of wilful murder was returned against him by the jury, with a strong recommendation to mercy, owing to the culprit having been at the time labouring under temporary insanity.

The learned judge who tried the case was

very severe on the police, whose duty in this instance had to be undertaken by civilians. On the other hand, he passed high encomiums upon Edwin and Carmel for the energy displayed in tracking and capturing the wretched man.

Easter Monday at Briar Town was ever a lively time, but on the present occasion, with the unusual attraction of the races in view, the town was so crowded that tents had to be erected by the hotel-keepers for the accommodation of their guests.

When the entries appeared, the committee had every reason to be satisfied with the result, the steeplechase being the event upon which the greatest interest centred, there being nine entries, viz.: Mr. Jackson's Bendigo; Mr. King's Fidget; Mr. Lindsay's Red Lancer; Mr. Cameron's Charcoal; Mr. Forrester's Douglas; Mr. Pearse's The Rover; Mr. McKay's Glenanlin; Mr. Gower's Borack; and Mr. Clancy's Bushranger.

The latter turned out to be Edwin's whilom captive, which it appeared the drover purchased from his rightful owner, a squatter on the Murrumbidgee.

The meeting between Edwin and Clancy was most cordial. It transpired that the latter's investment in land turned out a very profitable venture.

On the morning of Easter Monday, 185—, the scene at Briar Town was of the liveliest description. As early as eight o'clock horsemen came riding in, got up for the occasion, many, such as stock - riders and horse-breakers, being well mounted and clad chiefly in mole pants, Napoleon knee-boots, diggers' shirts, and cabbage-tree hats. Others, again, of the farming class, substituted white shirts for the more conspicuous red. Also could be seen sundry horse-carts, with mater and paterfamilias and a goodly number of olive - branches, all seemingly happy and joyous at the prospect of a day's outing.

The Briar Town society was represented by several carriages and dog-carts, but most of the young people preferred riding. Among the latter were our young friends from Tarragal and Baylup; also Yardly Mildman and his two sisters.

'I am glad to see you on horseback, Mildman,' said Carmel, 'as I promised to look after my sister and Miss Forrester; but, as much of my time will be occupied with the duties of starter, I shall put the ladies under your càre, and I hope you will just keep an eye on my sister's mare. She is very fresh this morning.'

'Very well, old fellow,' was the reply; 'I will constitute myself protector-general until you are disengaged, and in turn will stipulate that each of my fair charges will give me two waltzes this evening.'

'Oh, I am sure the fair charges will be very happy to do so,' said Ida. 'I do hope there will be lots of dancing gentlemen at the ball.'

A large crowd had by this time gathered on the course, and the rival publicans were doing a brisk trade, as were sundry ginger-beer stalls by the roadside. One happy family party might be seen making their way to the course in a dray, drawn by two bullocks, which were driven along at a trot, causing much amusement to the spectators, but not so to the unfortunate bullocks, to whom it was anything but a holiday.

The race-course was laid out on a beauti-

ful level plain bordering the creek, and
bounded on two sides by cornfields, the rank
stubble of which told of a prosperous harvest.
The straight run to the winning-post was
railed in, whilst the opposite side was a three-
railed fence, with a ditch, forming one side
of a lane leading to the burnt bridge before
mentioned.

At 11 a.m. the first bell was sounded, and
jockeys for the Maiden Plate weighed out.
The race was run in heats, and was won
easily by Carmel Murray's Dauntless, ridden
by Balgarra, who came to the scale grinning
from ear to ear.

The victory was a popular one, which
meant that the crowd must adjourn to the
booths and drink the health of the winner,
then of the rider, and afterwards their own.

The saddling-bell for the next race, however, caused a digression, and in a short
time it was known that a Tatiarra horse
had won the Publicans' Purse.   Next came
the Briar Town Plate, which fell to a local
farmer.   This led to another adjournment
to the booths.

An hour was now devoted to luncheon,

9

after which the competitors for the steeple-
chase put in an appearance, and in the
preliminary canter were keenly criticised.
The black horse Bushranger had many
admirers, and without doubt he was a
noble-looking animal, being sleek and well,
but a trifle too fleshy for a three-mile race.
Douglas also had a large body of supporters,
and numerous were the exhortations received
by Edwin as he passed down to the starting-
post.

'Now, Mr. Edwin, keep them going.
He can win if you give him his head.
Hooray for Mr. Forrester! I'll bet five
pounds on Master Edwin!' cried an old
farmer mounted on a carthorse; and the
cry was several times repeated along the
line.

Edwin was flushed and excited, as might
be expected, it being his first race in public.
His sisters were very persistent in their en-
treaties, begging him to be careful.

'You know, dear, how anxious mamma
will be,' said Nellie.

Mrs. Forrester would not venture on the
course, but spent the day at Baylup with

Mrs. Murray, who was suffering from an attack of neuralgia.

At length the anxious moment arrived, and the horses drew up in line at the starting-post.

'Now, then,' called Carmel, 'walk up steadily; keep back on Rover; forward Charcoal and Borack. Off!'

And down went the flag to an excellent start.

This race was three times round the course, over six fences each round, the first of which was outside the rails in front of the Steward's stand. This jump would be missed at the finish, as the horses would then keep on the running ground. The Rover led at the first fence, and cleared it in splendid style, closely followed by Glenanlin, ridden by a black boy. Red Lancer struck heavily and came down on his chest, but without unseating his rider, who recovered his horse instantly, amidst the cheers of the delighted spectators. The others got over without mishap, Douglas and Bushranger clearing the fence last, and side by side. At the second fence Fidget fell, and caused Bendigo to balk. Passing the stand the first time round the Rover still led, most of the horses taking their fences beautifully.

When passing the carriage-stand, Edwin waved his cap, with a smile, in response to the display of handkerchiefs; after which he took fourth place, still closely followed by his old rival the black. At the tenth fence the Rover came down, and got away from his rider, whilst at the twelfth Red Lancer and Glenanlin fell heavily, and were thus out of the hunt. Borack now held the lead, but only on sufferance, and as the last round was entered upon, Edwin improved the pace, Douglas going well within himself.

All through the race the scene within the course was one of wild excitement, each competitor being followed by a strong body of partisans, who galloped from leap to leap, cheering on their favourites; thus, while one party would be galloping westerly, others would be pursuing a northerly, and others again a southerly direction, which led to several collisions and many severe falls. The third fence from home was taken by Douglas and Bushranger simultaneously, followed at a distance by Borack, Charcoal, and Bendigo, in close order. The black horse, although jumping well, was getting winded. Edwin's confidence arose accordingly, and he took the lead at the next fence, Douglas taking it in his stride, whilst the black, close behind, struck the top rail heavily, but without a fall.

At this moment, Edwin's attention was attracted by a scream, followed by warning shouts, and casting his eyes to the left, the sight which met his gaze caused his heart to leap to his mouth. There he saw Fleet-wing coming down the lane at a frantic gallop, with her rider, hatless and pale, tugging in vain at the reins. Edwin saw at a glance that in a few seconds she must reach the burnt bridge, and then all would be over. With the speed of thought he wheeled Douglas, and put him at the fence bordering the lane ; but from the suddenness of the turn, or through throwing the horse out of his stride, Douglas broke the top rail, and failed to clear the ditch beyond, consequently he fell headlong into the lane, almost at the feet of Fleetwing, who stopped so suddenly that her rider was also thrown to the ground. Almost immediately about a dozen horsemen, who had started in pursuit of the runaway, arrived, and amongst them Carmel, Mildman, and Clancy; the former twain ran to the assistance of Edwin, who had not moved from where he fell, and whose head was already supported by the sobbing Ida.

Clancy, casting his eyes on the course, saw the black horse refuse the last fence, evidently through losing his leader. In less time than it takes to tell, the drover was on the back of Douglas, and sending him through the gap, was again on the course just as Borack and Charcoal had arrived at the spot. Only one hundred yards intervened between Clancy and the last fence, at which Bushranger had again balked; but at the next attempt, seeing his companions coming up, he cleared the fence, and his jockey sat down to ride him home, without looking round.

Giving no thought to the leader being his own property, Clancy sent Douglas at the leap full speed, and taking the fence in his stride, he landed five lengths behind the black, when he also sat down, and being no mean horseman, he rode for dear life at twenty yards from home, caught the leader, and squeezed Douglas past the post, the winner by a neck, amidst such excitement as was never before seen on a racecourse.

When the drover returned to scale he was found to be some pounds over weight, so that Douglas was declared the winner. When it became generally known that Clancy had beaten his own horse, the crowd seized him, and carrying him off shoulder-high, threatened to drown him in champagne.

We must now return to Edwin, whom we left lying in the lane, quite oblivious to the race and its results. Dr. Murray was soon on the spot, and finding his daughter safe, turned his attention to her preserver, and calling for some water, dashed it in his face, and in a few moments had the satisfaction of finding his patient open his eyes and ask, in a weak voice:

'What is the matter?'

'Don't talk now,' he was told. 'You have had a fall. My carriage will be here directly, when we will take you to Baylup.'

When the carriage arrived, a couch was formed with the cushions, and the patient driven steadily homeward, Nellie and Ida going in the carriage, the latter looking very pale and subdued, whilst Nellie's tears flowed freely.

No allusion was made to the accident by the ladies, in case of exciting the patient, who appeared to suffer great pain from the slight jolting of the carriage.

Carmel had ridden home in advance to apprise his mother of the accident, and to advise Mrs. Forrester of her son's state. The former lady at once set about putting a room in order, and by the time the carriage arrived all was ready to receive the injured youth.

Upon examination, it was found that the poor young fellow's right arm and three ribs were broken, as well as sundry bruises sustained. As quickly as possible the broken limb was set, and the other injuries attended to, when the patient expressed himself as much better, and begged his mother, who had

not left the bedside for a moment, to make
her mind easy on his account.

'Oh, my son, what should I have done if
you had been killed? You see, my fears
respecting that unlucky race were well
founded.'

'Well, you see, it was not the race, mother
dear; I should have been all right but for
Ida's mare taking the law in her own hands
and bolting off in that fashion. It makes my
blood run cold to think of her escape; it was
a near thing.'

'So I have heard, dear; but don't talk
any more just now. Dr. Murray says you
must keep quiet, and try to sleep. The
girls and I will watch by your bed to-night.'

'The girls, mother! why, are they not going
to the ball?'

'Oh no; they would not hear of such a
thing while you are so ill—besides, the
stewards have decided to postpone the ball
until to-morrow night.'

'I am glad of that, mother, as the girls
are tired and upset to-day, but they must all
go to-morrow evening.'

'Well, we will think about it by-and-by,

So now try and rest, dear;' and, getting
some knitting, the patient mother took her
seat beside the bed, from which she was
frequently called to answer anxious inquiries.

CHAPTER X.

HOW RACES ARE WON.

WE must now return to the racecourse, where we left the crowd all in excitement over the steeplechase. When matters had somewhat subsided, entries for the last race of the day were called ; this was for hacks, the property of farmers residing within thirty miles of the township. Now, as there were some 200 horsemen on the ground, and fifty per cent. of those had paid frequent visits to the shrine of Bacchus, almost every rider thought his horse could beat his neighbour's; consequently, there were twenty-eight entries for the race, which was to be run in heats, once round the course. Amongst the competitors might be seen an old acquaintance — the stockman, Cabbage-tree Bob, who, by the way, was quite in possession of his wits. He was mounted on a fine specimen of horseflesh, but rather fat for racing. A half-brother to the above was owned and ridden by Myall Sam; both were steel-grays and very much alike. Sam refused all persuasion to enter his horse, saying that there were too many in the race, and that he was afraid of getting his horse injured.

In due time, after a great deal of trouble, the stewards and starter managed to get the unruly lot away, amidst the yells and cheers of the multitude. By the time the leader had traversed half a mile, the different animals were strung out over a quarter of that distance, and ere the winning-post was reached, the tail was still further drawn out, several pulling up, whilst one rider came to grief, and his steed came galloping in amongst the ruck. The heat was won by Cabbage-tree Bob, who was hard pressed by Farmer Nolan's Tipperary.

For the second heat only twelve started, sundry bottles of square gin being wagered upon the result of the race between Nolan's chestnut and the steel-gray. These two had the race to themselves again, but the heat was won by Tipperary with ease at the finish, the gray being quite exhausted.

Long and loud were the shouts of the Tipperary boys at the result. Hats were thrown up, and a large amount of chaff indulged in at the stockman's expense, who, however, took it in good part, and returned it in kind.

'I say, Sam,' said the latter to his mate, 'we must turn the tables on these Tipperary boys, or we shall be chaffed out of the town. Come down to the brook and help me to wash my horse down a bit; it will freshen him up.'

'All right, Bob. Lead him on while I get a bucket.'

The two mates were seen shortly after throwing water over the horse, and diligently rubbing him down with some grass. After which Bob rode to the starting-post for the final heat, his horse still shivering from the effect of his douche.

'Why, Bob, what have you been doing with your horse? You will kill him, man,' said an acquaintance.

' Kill him, is it !' quoth a bystander.
' Faix, Tipperary will do that this minit.
Now, see if he don't ! Bedad, it's a feed of
oats the poor crathur wants, or a drop of
gin, sure !'

Five only faced the starter for the third
heat.

' Now thin, Patsey, you divil !' called out
a partisan to the rider of the chestnut ; ' put
the spurs into him from the start, and show
thim your tail all the way.'

At the fall of the flag Tipperary bounded
off with the lead, the gray keeping on his
quarter. Upon reaching the half-mile post,
Patsey applied the spurs as directed and
shot some three lengths ahead, to the delight
of his supporters ; but their joy was short-
lived, as the gray was slowly but surely
reducing the gap, and at the distance-post
had passed the chestnut and won the race
by two lengths, to the surprise of the spectators, who thought the horse quite done in
the second heat.

No sooner was the race decided than the
two stockmen withdrew quietly from the
crowd and took their way homewards, Bob

still riding the horse upon which he had won the race. After proceeding a mile or so, a clump of wattles appeared to the right of the road.

'I think we might as well go in there and change saddles,' said Sam. 'We may meet someone who will see through the joke.'

'Yes; the sooner the better. I am as pleased as if I owned a farm that I got to the windward of these Tipperary boys—not so much for the money, although that is a nice little sum ; but they would have chaffed us no end. That was a capital idea of ours to run a fresh horse for the third heat, and not a soul knew the difference.'

'Well, I think not; but I saw John Jackson eyeing him very sharply, but the cold-water business did the trick.'

From the foregoing conversation the reader will learn how the race was won. Cabbage-tree Bob ran his own horse for the first and second heats, and finding that he had no chance of winning the third, substituted his mate's fresh steed, with the result already shown. The change was effected at the brook, where they went ostensibly for the purpose of washing down the jaded animal, instead of which the water was thrown on the fresh horse, which was then saddled up and started. The scheme succeeded from its very boldness, and it was years before the secret leaked out. Had it transpired at the time, the country would have been made too hot to hold the perpetrators of the swindle.

The day following the races, Edwin found himself very stiff and unable to move, but otherwise in good spirits, and insisted upon his sister going to the race ball, which was to be the grandest affair of the kind ever held in the district.

When the Baylup party were dressed for the evening, they came in to show themselves to the invalid and wish him goodnight.

'I am so pleased to think that you are all going,' he remarked. 'You will have to excuse me, Miss Murray, for breaking my engagements.'

'Pray do not talk about it,' was the reply. 'Had it not been for your prompt and disinterested action, I should not have been here to fulfil mine. However, I shall keep your dances just as if you were there. So now good-night, and I hope you will rest well.'

The ball proved a great success; over one hundred tickets were sold, and dancing kept up until cock-crow. Yardly Mildman was in great form, and, being a good dancer, he had no difficulty in obtaining partners. Although the ladies were in the minority, Ida and Nellie were his partners on several occasions. This did not seem to please Carmel, who expressed his disapproval to his sister and her friend; and after a waltz with the latter, he invited his partner to a seat in the long veranda, which had been closed in for the occasion. Taking a seat beside her, he began:

' I have long been anxious to have a few words with you, Miss Forrester, and what I have seen this evening makes me still more anxious. I have often wished to tell you, but lacked the courage, that I love you very dearly, and have done so ever since I first saw you. Nay, do not go, Nellie, till you have heard me out,' as his partner attempted to rise. ' I think you know me to be truthful,

10

and I can assure you of my sincere devotion ; and if I can only be assured of your affection, it will give me new life. I have not much to marry upon, it is true, but with a little assistance from my father I could start a farm, where, with you for my wife, I should be as happy as a magpie at day-break.'

'I will not pretend that you have taken me by surprise, Mr. Murray ; but I am very sorry you told me what you did just now. I have always had the highest regard for you as my brother's friend, but have never thought of you in the light of a lover. Indeed, I have no intention of getting married at present. Come, let us get back to the ball-room ; our absence will be remarked.'

'One moment, pray,' was the reply. 'Have I been forestalled ? Are your affections already engaged ? Has that donkey Mildman worked his way into your good graces ? If I thought so I would—— But no '—clenching his hands—' I must not lose my head as well as my heart.'

'I cannot listen to your passionate tirade,

which is as unjust to Mr. Mildman as to myself, so will leave you to recover your temper at leisure; but let me tell you that when I marry, the man of my choice must have a comfortable home, and be possessed of sufficient means to keep a wife, for I have no intention of becoming a burden to my parents after marriage, like some ladies I could name.'

At this moment Yardly Mildman appeared, saying :

'Oh, Miss Forrester, I have been looking for you everywhere ; this is our dance ;' and, offering his arm, the pair were soon whirling round to the strains of a piano-and-violin gallop.

Upon the departure of his lady-love, Carmel betook himself to the hall, and, seizing his hat, started out into the night air, and after a brisk walk, returned to Baylup, where, seeing a light in Edwin's room, he looked in, and finding his friend awake, walked into the room.

'Well, old fellow, how has the ball turned out ? Is it over already ?'

'Oh no ; not nearly over yet. But I felt

inclined for a smoke, and having had dancing enough for one night, I came away.'

'But what about the ladies? I thought you were to bring them home? You know our governors will not sit up late, and they are relying upon you to do the needful. But you have not told me anything. I hope the girls are enjoying it?'

'Well, I suppose they are—that is, if dancing a lot is any criterion; they have been dancing all the evening with that empty-headed muff Mildman. I cannot see what there is in him for the girls to admire.'

'What is the matter, old man? has something put you out?'

'Well, look here, old fellow, I may as well tell you that I am in love with your sister, and she does not care a rush for me. I believe she cares very much more for Mildman, and he has been flirting with her all the evening, excepting while dancing with Ida. Why could he not have fallen in love with my sister instead of yours, then all would have been plain sailing. But what is the matter?' seeing Edwin wince; 'are you in pain?'

'Yes, rather,' was the reply; 'my arm gives me a twinge occasionally; but you don't think that Ida cares for the fellow, do you?'

'Well, she seemed to like dancing with him, at all events, and there is no accounting for tastes. For my own part, I am left out in the cold.'

'Don't get a fit of the blues, old man; just fancy that you are as good a man as anyone else; keep up your spirits, and all will come right in the end.'

'Well, perhaps I am a muff; at any rate, I will return to the ball-room and see the ladies home.'

So saying, he retraced his steps, leaving Edwin to commune with himself on the subject of the late discourse, the result of which he found it idle to speculate upon. So, taking a sleeping draught from his ever-anxious mother, he was soon in a slumber, in which he saw Ida carried off by Yardly Mildman, who had assumed the shape of an old-man-kangaroo. In the excitement of the supposed chase he awoke with a start to find day just breaking, and shortly after his mother appeared with a cup of beef-tea.

'Well, mother, what time did the dancers return?' was his first question.

'About three o'clock,' was the reply—'shortly after I left you; they appear to have enjoyed the ball very much, and to have had lots of dancing.'

'Yes, so I heard from Carmel last night. Poor fellow, he was rather in the dumps, and is under the impression that Nellie treated him badly—in fact, slighted him in favour of Yardly Mildman, who, between ourselves, is not to be compared to Murray in any way.'

'Well, really, my dear, I am somewhat in a maze! Do you think that Carmel cares for Nellie otherwise than as a friend? They always have appeared like brother and sister.'

'Oh yes, that is all very well; but I fear the brother-and-sister business won't last much longer; in fact, Carmel admitted to me last night that he was in love with Nellie, and felt much annoyed at the attention paid her by Mildman.'

'Well, really, I suppose I ought to have been prepared for something of the kind;

but Nellie has always seemed to me a child, and I had no thought of anyone falling in love with her just yet. However, I will talk with her on the subject, although at present neither young Mildman nor Carmel would be in a position to marry.'

The opportunity for the proposed confidential talk did not immediately present itself, as Mr. Forrester and Nellie started for Tarragal shortly after breakfast, Mrs. Forrester remaining to take care of her son, who remained on the sick-list for nearly a fortnight. Ida was Mrs. Forrester's chief assistant in nursing the invalid, and spent an hour every evening reading to him. Her arrival in the room was like a beam of sunshine on a winter's day, and she never came empty-handed. First, there would be some fresh roses for his table; again, the weekly paper would be brought in, and portions of the latest news read out, one paragraph of which interested our hero very much.

This was an account of the loss of a party of brave explorers, who some years before had started out, full of hope, into the wilds of the interior, bound for Western Australia;

but from the time of leaving the last cattle-station on Liverpool Plains, they had never been heard of, although from time to time search parties had been despatched in quest of the missing men. It was supposed that the leader, who was a man of indomitable perseverance, had perished, and that his men, or at any rate a portion of them, were now living with the blacks in the far-away interior. The article published suggested that a strong party should be despatched by the Governments of New South Wales, Victoria, and South Australia, and invited volunteers to offer their services for the expedition.

As might be expected, our hero was much interested in the thrilling accounts which set forth how the names of the gallant rescuers would be handed down to posterity, in addition to which untold wealth in the shape of an undiscovered goldfield might at any moment cross their path.

After this event, Edwin could talk of nothing else, much to the alarm of his mother, who dreaded the thought of her beloved son leaving her for the purpose of undergoing such unheard-of perils. Mrs. Murray and Ida also deprecated the idea of any young men who had friends who loved them venturing out upon such a wild-goose chase. Fortunately, they thought, Carmel was absent, having gone to attend a cattle muster at a neighbouring station, and would not return before Edwin's contemplated departure for Tarragal, which was arranged to take place in a day or two.

CHAPTER XI.

A WEEK after the ball Edwin received the following letter from his friend:

'Baylup, *April*, 185-.

'DEAR EDWIN,

'I am getting sick of this humdrum life, and have made up my mind to strike out for myself; therefore think I shall volunteer for service with John McDouall Stuart, or some other plucky explorer, and seek adventure in a new and distant land where a fellow can find elbow-room. We are getting crowded out in this neighbour-hood, and there is no chance for a young fellow to make anything, especially with the limited capital at my disposal. This place is becoming unbearable, and only fit for that young cad Mildman, with his English airs which seem to be so much admired by the ladies; although I can't see what there is to admire in the fellow, except that he can dance and play cricket better than most of us. But enough of this grumbling.. If you would only make up your mind to go out with me, I should be happy; and seriously, I believe we should make a good thing by taking up a large block of new country, and starting a sheep station. Just look at those Robertsons, who started only four years ago on the Upper Darling with only 2,000 sheep! They have now 7,000, with a magnificent run, and are in a fair way of making a large fortune. I wish you would ride over, old fellow, some evening, and let us talk the matter over. I would come and see you, but cannot, for reasons known to you.

'I am, dear Edwin,

'Your sincere friend,

'CARMEL MURRAY.'

The contents of Carmel's letter afforded the recipient thereof food for thought during the evening. He broached the subject to his father, saying that with the latter's per-

mission he felt inclined to seek his fortunes
in a new country.

'For you know, father,' said ⬛, 'we
are getting pretty well crowded out down
here. Why, in a ⬛ears the whole of
your run will be in the hands of Cockatoo
farmers; then your oc⬛ation will be gone.'

'There is reason in your observations, my
boy, and perhaps, were you a year or two
older, I should ⬛t object to your striking
out a line for yourself, but this expedition of
Stuart's in search of Leichar⬛ although it
is a very commendable und⬛ing, and has
my entire sympathy—is not likely to prove
profitable to the undertakers; therefore, I
should advise you to wait awhile, and when
opportunity occurs, I shall be ready to assist
you in any suitable enterprise; and if you
can persuade Carmel to renounce his present
intention, so much the better, for when you
do leave home I should like him to join you,
as I have a high opinion of that young
fellow's energy and ability. He is bound to
make his way.'

'Well, father, it will perhaps be better, as
you say, to wait awhile. I wish you would

kindly pen a few lines to Carmel for me in reply. My arm is too stiff just yet for writing.'

' Very well ; I will drop him a line and ask him to come over and see us, when we can discuss the subject. I am rather surprised that he did not ride over instead of writing to you. Why, really, now I come to think of it, ˴he has not been here since the races. Surely he has not taken a dislike to any of us !'

' Oh, not at all ; he is down in the dumps, poor fellow, that is all. Katie has been begging for a picnic for some time, so I tell you what we will do. We'll get the mater to ask our friends from around Briar Town for some day next week, then we will take the carriages out to Kangaroo Flat with the necessaries of life, and have a grand kangaroo hunt.'

The ladies were soon called together, and all highly approved of the arrangement, especially Katie, who had not yet got over the annoyance of not seeing the ball. However, she vowed she would make up for the disappointment by having a real good run after a boomer.

In due time a reply came from Mrs. Murray and the Parsonage, accepting the invitation to the picnic, Mrs. Murray adding that she would take the liberty of bringing two young officers who were spending a few days at Baylup, where they had arrived with a letter of introduction to Dr. Murray from an old schoolfellow, who was now medical officer on board H.M.S. *Emu*, which had run into port a few days previously, and would be detained a few days repairing damages.

The evening preceding the eventful day, a large party gathered around Mrs. Forrester's table, and passed the time with whist, music, and dancing. The two young officers soon won golden opinions, being both very agreeable young fellows, and seemed as happy as schoolboys out for a holiday. Carmel, although at first he had declined the invitation, was persuaded to be one of the party, and was very pleased with the amusing anecdotes of the young officers, whose names, by the way, were Thomson and Mainstay, the former a lieutenant, and the latter, a youth of seventeen, holding the rank of midshipman.

Arrived at the Kangaroo Flat, where the dogs had been sent some hours before, girths were tightened, and a start made for the hunting-ground, several ladies being of the party—Ida on this occasion being mounted on a quiet pony, whilst her brother rode Fleetwing; Edwin was also reduced to a quiet old stock horse, intending to follow the chase quietly. The two sailors were provided with good steady mounts. Lieutenant Thomson proved to be a very fair horseman, but the midshipman's horse carried him just where he pleased, much to the amusement of the ladies, who quizzed the young sailor unmercifully, all of which he took in good part.

'There they go!' cried Carmel; and immediately all were in a gallop in pursuit of a mob of kangaroos, and as the country was clear, dogs as well as game were in full view. Mainstay entered eagerly into the spirit of the chase, and, throwing his reins on the horse's neck, clapped his hands and hallooed the dogs, at the same time rolling about all over the saddle. The horse, being accustomed to the sport, singled out a boomer that had broken off to the left, and pursued him closely until entering some brushwood covered with a vine-like creeper, when the luckless midshipman found himself hung up by the middle, and had the mortification of seeing his horse continue the chase on his own account; but after a short gallop he left the boomer and rejoined his equine companions, where the party were grouped around a large kangaroo, who stood at bay and defied both dogs and hunters. Carmel dismounted, and breaking off a sapling, walked up to the boomer, and with a well-directed blow, delivered behind the ears, brought the monster to earth, when, seizing him by the tail, he, with a pocket-knife, severed the ham-strings, thus rendering the animal powerless to inflict injury with the deadly claws with which his toes were armed. Attention was now directed to the midshipman's horse, and fears were entertained for the rider's safety; but these were soon dispelled by the appearance of Mainstay running in their direction. Upon arrival, he created much amusement by a description of his accident.

After another cast around, in which three
more kangaroos were despatched, the hunters
and huntresses returned to camp and enjoyed an *al fresco* repast, with appetites
sharpened by the morning's work, after
which they returned in high spirits to Tarragal. The young sailors could talk of nothing
but their hair-breadth escapes, and vowed
that no life could compare with that of an
Australian squatter.

During the day the lieutenant kept in
close attendance upon Nellie, as in duty
bound, she being his host's eldest daughter,
whilst Katie, much to her ladyship's delight,
had a devoted admirer in the midshipman,
the pair keeping up an incessant chatter, and
making noise enough for the whole party.
Ida constituted herself Edwin's caretaker,
saying that as his accident was caused
through her carelessness, she must make
what amends she could. This, however, did
not suit Yardly Mildman, who, ever since the
ball, had thrown himself as much as possible
in Ida's way, and during the hunt had scarcely
left her side, much to the annoyance of

Edwin, who would have much preferred a *tête-à-tête* ride.

After tea, Mr. Forrester opened the topic of exploration, and all were soon engrossed in the subject; Carmel expressing' himself strongly in favour of joining Stuart's expedition, whilst Mr. Forrester and Edwin were in favour of seeking new country on their own account, without being tied down to a certain line of action. The ladies objected most strongly to the idea, which, they reasoned, would lead to no good result, and were never tired of pointing out the dangers to be encountered from untamed savages, fever and ague, death from thirst, and the thousand-and-one ills to which explorers are subject. On the other hand the gentlemen all supported the motion, and sat up until past midnight discussing ways and means ; the result being that Mr. Forrester was induced to give a reluctant consent to Edwin's going out so soon as he recovered from the effects of his late accident. He also promised to ride over to Baylup in a few days and to talk the matter over with Mr. Murray.

After spending two very happy days at Tarragal, the young sailors took leave of the Forresters, vowing that they would return some day and settle down in Australia. Carmel 'and Ida also departed, the former having had an opportunity of clearing up the misunderstanding existing between himself and Nellie.

According to promise, Mr. Forrester shortly put in an appearance at Baylup, and had a long conversation with Mr. Murray, the result of which was that their sons should be sent out to Arnheim's Land, in the North-west portion of Australia, where good grazing country was supposed to exist, and in the event of the preliminary survey turning out satisfactorily, a large tract of country should be secured, and stock sent over.

CHAPTER XII.

THE ATTACK.

On December 15, 185–, a party consisting of four horsemen might have been seen wending their way over a stony plain in the far interior of North-west Australia. The day was sultry in the extreme, and the tropical sun shot its vertical rays upon their heads. The riders consisted of three white men and one black, the former being well-tanned by exposure to the weather. Each horseman was armed with a rifle or double-barrelled carbine, whilst four pack-horses were laden with the necessaries of life, rugs, etc. A canvas water-bag suspended from each saddle hung limp and shrivelled, showing the absence of the life-giving fluid, more precious than gold to the brave pioneer who treads the trackless wilds, and who may truly be said to carry his life in his hand.

After some distance had been traversed, the leader reined up, and, turning to his nearest companion, said:

'I fear, Edwin, the horses will not hold out much longer, unless we find water. It is now twenty-four hours since the poor brutes had a drink.'

'Yes, and I opine it will go rather hard with ourselves also. I would give a guinea for a quart of water just now. Unless we strike some within an hour, I vote we retrace our steps to the Cajeput spring passed yesterday.'

'Let us have Balgarra's opinion,' said Carmel (the reader will doubtless have guessed who our friends are). 'His black wit may probably suggest something.'

The appeal was made, but in vain, Balgarra being as helpless in this new land as his white brethren. The fourth member of the party, who was no other than our acquaintance Dick Evans, did not offer an opinion, but waited patiently to learn what course his companions intended to pursue.

' Well,' said Carmel, ' I vote we make over to that clump of gums and wait for the cool of the evening, and then push on for that range away to the north during the night.'

This resolve was acted upon, and the weary travellers at length reached the welcome shade referred to, when saddles were removed and the jaded horses hobbled out. The riders soon spread their rugs, and reclined at full length on the parched earth, where they in vain tried to pass the hours in sleep, but a great thirst was now upon them, which put sleep out of the question. (I may here state, that having induced the elder Messrs. Murray and Forrester to consent to an exploring tour, the young men elected to strike out on their own account, and therefore took passage for themselves and horses by a barque which had been chartered to proceed from Melbourne to Dampier's Archipelago, for the purpose of getting a cargo of guano from one of the many islands upon which such deposits were known to exist. Our friends were landed on the coast of Arnheim's Land, with the understanding that they were to be picked up by the

Mohawk on her return, which was supposed to be in about two months' time. But to return to our travellers.)

On the evening in question the sun set like a ball of fire, just as our friends had saddled up.

'I tell you what it is,' said Carmel; 'we shall have a storm before many hours are over, or I am much mistaken. I saw just such a sunset once in the West Indies, and before we knew where we were we had a cyclone that nearly blew our craft out of the water.'

'I trust in Heaven you may be right,' said Edwin, 'as the wind would most likely bring rain.'

The party had now started, and Edwin, who was in the van, had proceeded about a quarter of a mile when, in crossing a small ravine, he saw a bronze-winged pigeon fly up a short distance to the right. Calling out to his companions that there must be water near, he rushed off, and in twenty seconds saw the most welcome sight it had ever been his fortune to witness, viz., a nice pool of transparent fresh water, with the margin fringed with drooping palms. Men and horses soon had their heads in the water, the former not waiting to unstrap panni-kins.

In a short time the horses were again un-saddled, and our friends prepared to cook their evening meal and form camp for the night.

After an excellent supper, composed chiefly of bream taken from the pool by Balgarra, the night-watch was set, and three of the weary travellers were soon wrapped in slumber.

Long before daybreak breakfast was ready, and Dick, who had the morning-watch, called his companions. To enable the stock of flour to spin out, it had been arranged that what is known as skilly, viz., flour boiled with water, seasoned with a little sugar, should form breakfast when no game was at hand, and on this occasion Dick made his first attempt at cooking the new dish.

' I don't know what to make of this here skilly, Master Edwin,' he said; ' I've been stirring it for the last hour, but it won't get thick.'

' Why not ? How much water have you in the billy ?'

' Oh, not above six or seven quarts,' was the reply. ' And I put in the small pannikin full of flour, just as you told me.'

' Good gracious!' cried Edwin; ' what a head you must have. Why, how do you think it possible that half a pint of flour could thicken six quarts of water? I fear, Dick, we must not trust you to cook break-fast again.'

By sunrise a start was made in the direc-tion of the high range seen the day before, which was reached by mid-day, and a spring of water discovered in a gorge, hemmed in by stupendous cliffs on two sides. Around the spring was some luxuriant grass, upon which the horses were soon browsing.

It was resolved to rest the horses here for half a day; accordingly Balgarra took his gun—as was his usual practice—and started away to hunt for game.

' Do not go far away,' called Carmel. ' I see there are fresh tracks of natives about, and you might get a spear-wound if you are not careful.'

'Oh, me nothing frightened fellow. Suppose blackfellow throw 'em spear, me quickfellow shootem two or three.'

'You must do nothing of the kind,' he was told, 'but look out and keep clear of any natives whilst out alone.'

In less than an hour Balgarra returned with two rock kangaroo, which he threw down; then, resting his gun against a rock, he commenced to pluck the fur off his game, and otherwise prepare it for cooking.

'Well, Balgarra,' said Carmel, 'have you seen any blackfellows?'

'Nothing blackfellow seeum; but plenty track get down, all same flock sheep. Look here, what you callem this fellow?' taking a peculiar lump of stone from his pocket and showing it to the young men.

'By heavens! *gold!*' cried both in a breath. 'Where did you find that?'

The sample in question was a mixture of trap rock and quartz, thickly impregnated with gold. The specimen was passed around, drawing exclamations of surprise and delight from all hands.

A discussion was at once raised as to

following up Balgarra's discovery, and it was decided that next morning two of the party should take care of the camp, whilst the others made a search for the precious metal.

'What a grand thing it would be if we should discover another Bendigo or Eagle-hawk in this land of the West!' said Edwin. 'I wonder whether the Swan River Government will give us a reward for our discovery?'

'I should not count much upon that,' replied Carmel. 'I have heard my father say that it is a poor place, only populated in the south-west corner of the colony by about twenty thousand people, where the Governor is Prime Minister, Comptroller of Convicts, etc., and in fact has unlimited authority. An old schoolfellow of my father's was Governor of the colony for five years, and by his account he had autocratic powers; so that I should say it would be unwise to count upon a Government reward where no Government exists.'

As neither Carmel nor Edwin cared to remain in camp next day, it was decided that the whole party should proceed to the spot where Balgarra made the discovery, taking horses and outfit with them for safety. Upon reaching the spot, a small rocky gully abounding with quartz and schist, a vigorous but unsuccessful search was made, and by noon our friends returned to the spring, exhausted and somewhat dis-heartened, but determined to try again the next morning.

A large emu was shot by Balgarra whilst coming to water, and a portion of the meat was cut into strips and dried in the sun for future use.

'What would the Briar Town people say, could they see us now?' said Edwin. 'Why, our friends would not recognise us, and would certainly not envy us our repast of damper and emu.'

'Well, I suppose not, old fellow; still, there is something exciting and pleasant in this free, out-door life—especially when you feel that you are travelling over country never before pressed by the foot of civilized man.'

'Yes, I agree with you that there is a ,

certain amount of pleasure and excitement about this life ; but as to civilized man never having seen this country, that is more than we can say. Why, the fact of our find of gold goes to prove that some portion of this country must have been known at least two centuries ago. My father has a work of very old date, giving an account of Dutch discoveries along this coast in the seventeenth century, wherein the voyagers describe the land as *terra-aurifera*, so that they must have found gold in this neighbourhood.'

' I think that is very likely,' replied Carmel ; ' but I don't think for a moment that those Dutch sailors ever left the coast-line. At any rate, being without horses, they were not at all likely to have come four hundred miles inland, which is about our distance from the coast to-day.'

The next morning another start was made for Golden Gully, and on this occasion some earth was scraped together, and carried in pack-bags to the spring, and there washed out in the billy generally used for boiling meat, the result being that three minute colours were obtained for the day's work.

Whilst seated in the shade of a huge baobab - tree, regaling themselves upon damper and tea, Balgarra uttered a low stockman's whistle, which immediately put all hands on the alert, and, looking up, a blackfellow and two gins were seen approaching the spring, following down the ravine, with their eyes, as usual, cast on the ground. They came up leisurely to within twenty yards of our friends, when some slight noise attracted the man's attention. He looked up, and for half a moment all three remained spellbound ; then, uttering an unearthly yell, and crying to the women to retire, he shipped a long reed spear, taken from a bundle in his left hand, and taking a position between the travellers and his wives, retreated slowly with his face to the enemy, keeping up a constant fire of directions to his companions, who were almost powerless from fear.

The moment they were observed, our friends stood up and endeavoured to make known their friendly intentions, hoping to induce the natives to approach so that they might make friends of them. This, however, could not be done, as whenever one of the whites walked forward, the naked warrior advanced to meet him with elevated spear, tapping his shield on his haunch the while. At length, having reached some large rocks, the savages dodged behind them, and setting off at a run, were soon out of sight.

'I tell you what it is, Mr. Edwin,' said Dick; 'I'm thinking we'd better clear out from here pretty quick, or that big beggar will be here with a mob, and make dead meat of us all. I always thought they were cannibals up this way, and now I am sure on it. Didn't you see how he stared at us and shook that spear?'

'Well, Dick, I think your advice has some merit in it, and it will be wise to follow it, although we have no reason to count upon the hostility of the blacks; and I am sure we have as yet no reason for crediting them with cannibalism. If they try a slice of you for dinner, Dick, I think they will find you a tough morsel.'

'Aye, I'll bet they will; and they'll find me a tough customer to kill, too. I reckon my old horse-pistol has a dozen good slugs in her, anyway.'

'Well, let us hope there will be no occasion to use your firelock.   There is no doubt that the poor fellow we saw was terribly frightened.'

Before sunset, horses were saddled and preparations made for a start, when a shout was heard up the ravine, and looking in that direction, our travellers saw over twenty warriors, fully armed with spear, shield and boomerang, advancing towards them in war-like attitude.   The word was at once given to mount, in case of a rush.   The riders now faced the natives, making friendly signs ; but ignoring these, the wilgied savages ran up to within range and discharged a shower of spears, most of which fell short; one, how-ever, inflicted a skin-wound upon one of the pack-horses, which caused the poor brute to plunge about.

'We must fire a shot,' cried Carmel, ' or those brutes will do us harm.   I will let go over their heads.'

Accordingly he fired his fowling-piece, the report of which reverberated loudly along the cliffs.

OUR FRIENDS FOUND SPEARS FALLING AMONGST THEM.

Page 177.

The effect was magical. Several warriors fell flat on their faces, whilst others commenced scaling the cliffs, whither their prostrate companions soon followed them.

After assembling, they appeared to compare notes, and finding that none of their party were hurt, they advanced along the top of the cliffs, and again prepared to attack.

'Me thinkum we must quickfellow walk,' said Balgarra excitedly. 'That way too many blackfellow come on. Me plenty seeum other side hill get down.'

Upon looking in the direction indicated, the travellers observed a large party of blacks gathering on the opposite cliffs, so that they were now between two fires. The horses were at once put in motion, and proceeding at a trot over the stony ground, the friends hoped to soon get beyond reach of danger. However, this retreat was the signal for hostilities to commence, and our friends again found spears falling amongst them. Two shots were now fired from the fowling-pieces, with the hope that some smart shot-wounds would cause the blacks to beat a retreat, but unfortunately it had the opposite effect. Redoubling their yells, they again discharged a shower of spears, one of which penetrated Carmel's arm, giving him a serious wound, whilst a boomerang knocked off Dick Evans' hat.

CHAPTER XIII.

TO THE RESCUE.

EDWIN now fired his rifle, and a black, who was conspicuous by his boldness, fell backwards from his position. Balgarra also brought down a man with his carbine. These two shots to some extent checked the onslaught, and caused the blacks to retire a short distance, keeping up a most discordant noise the while.

Edwin at once rushed to the assistance of his friend, who was in great pain and very faint; the ugly barbed spear still stuck through his arm, the shaft or reed portion having fallen off at the socket. Edwin with his knife cut the wood off close to the arm, then drew the spear out, and bound the arm with his handkerchief, saying:

'Courage, old man; we shall soon be out

of this gorge, when we can easily beat off those black demons.'

No sooner had the friends started again than their foes rallied and began descending the cliffs. Edwin and Balgarra faced round, determined to check the savages, and enable Carmel to work his way out of the ravine with Dick and the horses. As the natives came on two more shots were fired, and two more dusky forms dropped their spears, but the rest pushed on, yelling like fiends. Edwin, casting his eyes round, saw that his companions with the pack-horses were almost clear of the gorge, so, giving the word to Balgarra, the two urged their horses to their best speed, which, considering the rocky nature of the gorge, was only a slow canter, but they knew that once round the next bend they would reach the open plain, when their pursuers would be easily left behind.

Shouting to Carmel and Dick, ' Push on, another moment will put us in safety!' to his surprise Edwin saw Dick, who was in the lead, suddenly turn back and stop Carmel, shouting at the same time: ' Look! look! the black devils have surrounded us,' and to his dismay Edwin saw over a score of warriors barring their passage to the open plain.

The four riders were soon together, and a hurried consultation was held as to the best course to pursue, when it was resolved to charge the party in front, firing as many shots as possible to scare the savages: the pack-horses were to be left to work their way out as best they might, it being certain that they would follow their fellows.

Carmel's wound was now very painful, but the excitement kept him up for the time.

Balgarra's black blood was up, and his eyes fairly glistened with rage. No sooner was the word given than he dashed at the crowd of savages, and warding off a spear with the barrel of his carbine, he shot his aggressor. Then, rushing his horse at another, he knocked him over, and the next moment found himself clear and outside the ranks, with Edwin close behind—the latter having wounded two of his assailants with a discharge of his double-barrel. Carmel and Dick, however, had not fared so well, the former having been knocked off his horse

with the blow of a dowark, whilst the latter
had his horse speared in the flank so badly
that the poor brute spun round and fell over
on its side, the rider fortunately falling clear ;
but before he was fairly on his legs, a lusty
savage rushed at him with uplifted club,
and Dick's hours would certainly have been
numbered had he not retained possession of
his horse-pistol, which he fired point-blank,
and had the satisfaction of seeing his enemy
bite the dust.

No sooner did Edwin see his friend on the
ground than, calling on Balgarra and Dick,
he again charged the blacks, but by this time
the whole of the sable warriors had descended
from the cliffs, and were fast closing in ; the
fallen man all this time lay without the
slightest sign of life, and a great fear seized
Edwin that his friend was dead. He called
his name loudly, but received no response ;
the blacks also appeared to think him dead,
and turned their attention to their living
foes, again discharging their spears to
such purpose that the distracted Edwin
and his companions found it impossible to
get near the fallen Carmel without courting

certain death, particularly as they had not an opportunity of reloading their firearms.

In an instant our hero took in the situation, and resolved to beat a retreat, and if possible draw the blacks out on the plain ; so, giving the word, the three riders turned their horses' heads, and in a short time found themselves in the open country, still pursued by the whole host of natives.

They now reloaded and fired a volley, which took effect, and brought a reply of spears, etc. Edwin now gathered up his horses, and still keeping out of reach of danger, drew the blacks on until they were fully half a mile out on the plain. Then, catching Carmel's horse, and setting off at a gallop, he made a circuit, and dashed away for the ravine, determined to recover his friend if alive.

Upon nearing the spot, his delight may be imagined when he saw Carmel sitting up, but looking very pale, with blood flowing from a wound in his temple.

Edwin was on the ground in an instant.

' How are you, old fellow ? I was afraid they had done for you. Are you much hurt ?'

'Water,' was the only response.

Snatching a water-bag off the saddle, he held it to the wounded man's lips, who drank greedily, after which he seemed much relieved.

'Now then, old man,' said Edwin; 'let me help you on your horse. We must be out of the pass before the black brutes return. I left Dick and Balgarra to keep them in play as long as possible.'

With some difficulty Carmel was mounted, and, Edwin leading the wounded man's horse, a start was made, and in a few minutes, much to Edwin's relief, the open plain was reached. Putting their horses to a canter, they soon came up with their companions, who had halted at a safe distance from where the blacks had also come to a standstill, having at last realized their inability to outrun their mounted foes.

Wet bandages were now applied to Carmel's wounds, after which our friends departed in haste, returning on their tracks to Palm Spring, where they all were glad to avail themselves of a much-needed rest; the wounded man especially being very much exhausted, whilst his companions all evinced the greatest solicitude on his account.

'Now, old man,' said Edwin, 'lie down on this rug and try and have a sleep, whilst we make some tea. I don't think those black demons will follow us this far; at any rate, if they do we can see their approach over the plain.'

As night approached, water-bags were filled, and a move made onwards, as it was not considered safe to camp so near the enemy at night.

Three weeks later found our friends on the sea coast, Carmel having quite recovered. Upon inspecting the signal-station, they found that the barque had not returned from the islands, therefore they commenced to build a small stone hut, which would shelter them from the sun's rays, and likewise be some protection in case of an attack by natives. Here a week was spent very pleasantly, game and fish being abundant, and grass growing most luxuriantly around the spring, so that the horses were rapidly putting on flesh.

'It will be rather awkward,' remarked

Carmel, 'should the *Mohawk* come to grief
on one of those coral reefs mentioned by
the skipper. We have only about another
fortnight's rations left.'

'Well, I see no use in anticipating mis-
fortunes,' replied Edwin. 'Should the vessel
not turn up soon, we must try and make
overland to Swan River. I recollect reading
that about fifteen years ago Sir George
Grey, having been wrecked somewhere up
this way, made his way overland to Perth, on
foot, with his boat's crew. If he got through,
why should not we?'

'That is all very well; but Grey had not
so far to travel. However, there is still time
for our *Mohawk* to show up, so we will sleep
on the subject.'

At daybreak next morning Balgarra, as
usual, ascended an adjacent hillock, and no
sooner had he gained the summit than he
cooeed and waved his hat, upon which all
hands picked up their firearms and were
soon beside him, when to their delight they
saw the barque anchored about four miles
off shore. A fire was soon lit, and at short
intervals a second and third, this being the

NO SOONER HAD HE GAINED THE SUMMIT THAN HE COOEED.

Page 186.

signal agreed upon. The signal was quickly responded to by the report of a gun and the hoisting of a flag.

Our friends now returned to their camp, and prepared what they hoped would be their last breakfast on shore; after discussing which they packed up their traps and carried them down to the shore, in readiness for the long-boat, now making its way shorewards. It had been decided to turn the horses adrift, as the expense of taking them back to Melbourne would be more than they were worth when landed there.

Upon nearing the shore the captain, who was a jovial young fellow, leaped on land, and shook hands warmly with the explorers, saying:

'I am right glad to see you all safe and sound. How did you get on? Find lots of good sheep country, eh? Were the darkies at all troublesome?'

'We may say "Yes" to both queries,' he was told; 'but we shall have lots of time to recount our adventures on board. How did you fare at the islands?'

'Oh, very fairly; I got a full cargo at last,

but only by working day and night. But come along, let us get on board and under way.'

By noon the good ship *Mohawk* spread her sails to the breeze, and shaped a course for the North-west Cape, which was sighted in due course, and a fresh departure taken for Cape Leeuwin, which they hoped to reach in about ten days. The production of Balgarra's nugget gave rise to various tales of Dutch discoveries, and their attempts at founding new settlements.

'In our present latitude, and not many miles to the eastward,' said the captain, 'is a large island, upon which they landed, calling it after that venturesome old sailor, Dirk Hartog; and further south is a group of islands named after one Houtman; they are better known as Houtman's Abrolhos. On this group somewhere in the last century a large treasure-ship was lost. The crew mutinied, with the view, it is supposed, of getting possession of the gold, which they hid so effectually that it has never been discovered. The mutineers, who were afterwards brought away and executed, refused to divulge the secret.'

'Was the treasure never searched for sub-
sequently?' inquired Edwin.

'Oh yes, on several occasions; but it is
not known on which of the numerous islands
it is hidden, so that for the last seventy or
eighty years nothing has been done in the
matter, and there is no doubt but that a
hillock of sand now covers many a spot that
in those days was as level as this deck, which
would necessarily lessen the chance of discovering the plant.   But I must go on deck
and reduce sail, as the wind is rising.'

In a short time the watch was ordered
away to take in canvas, and soon the
barque was under easy sail, and the captain,
having returned to the saloon, ordered some
hot whisky, which was discussed, after which
our landsmen turned in, and were soon
wrapped in slumber.

When morning broke Edwin made his
way on deck and found a very high sea
running, with a strong westerly wind, which
came with great force across the Indian
Ocean.   The captain, who was pacing the
deck, replied to our hero's question about
the weather:

'Well, yes, it is blowing a bit stiffish; but we have a good offing, so there is nothing to fear.'

Towards night the gale increased, and the wind, veering round to the south-west, brought up a jumpy cross sea, which caused the *Mohawk* to pitch and roll about considerably, the extra motion making matters somewhat uncomfortable for our landsmen.

All through the night the gale continued without abatement, the barque carrying now only sufficient canvas to give her steerage-way.

'I say, Edwin,' cried Carmel, from the top bunk of their joint cabin, 'this is worse than over-landing, with a few savages thrown in!'

'Well, it is quite bad enough,' was the reply; 'but I hope the worst is over, as the captain says the gale should blow itself out to-day.'

In another moment the speaker found himself on the floor, the vessel having struck heavily and turned over on her side. On deck all was confusion, the concussion having

THE WAVES WASHED OVER THE DOOMED HULL.

Page 191.

sent both fore and mainmast over the side, whilst the waves washed over the doomed hull and passed away to leeward in seething foam over the jagged reef upon which the ill-fated ship had struck.

CHAPTER XIV.

THE WRECK.

By the time our hero and Carmel reached the deck, they found the captain and most of the crew gathered together on the poop, clinging on to anything they could get hold of. The port quarter boat was under water, therefore the captain turned his attention to the gig, which hung on the starboard davits, and gave orders to lower away. This was accomplished with some difficulty, but no sooner had the boat touched the water than a monster wave dashed with great force against the ship's side, completely wrecking the boat; and, not satisfied with the mischief done, the wave swept the deck, carrying away Edwin and two of the sailors, whom he had been assisting at the tackles. In the darkness and confusion the men were

not for the moment missed, but a heart-rend-
ing shriek from one of the doomed men
notified to those on the wreck that some of
their number had gone to their last account.
Carmel quickly missed his friend, and was
well-nigh distracted. He called his name
repeatedly, in the vain hope that he might
still be on board, but was soon convinced
that such hope was futile.

'Oh, my more than brother!' he cried;
'we shall soon follow you.'

In the meantime, the captain gave orders
that all hands should mount the mizzen
rigging, and there wait for daylight, should
the vessel hold together so long. In this
perilous position they clung for over an
hour, when the welcome streak of light
announcing dawn appeared in the east; and
when the sun rose the high mainland could
be made out some twenty-five miles distant, whilst to the south-east and south,
scarcely a mile off, could be seen several low
islands, over which swarms of sea-birds were
flying in various directions.

To reach those islands seemed their only
hope, and to do this a raft must be con-

structed. As the sun came out the wind lulled, and by noon the sea had calmed down considerably; the stern of the vessel was now fairly dry, and the wearied crew descended to the deck. The first thing to be done was to see what eatables were available, and after a search, the steward found some ships' biscuit and rum, upon which the half-famished men regaled themselves.

Carmel and the black boy were terribly cut up at the loss of Edwin, poor Balgarra sobbing out his grief in a most pitiable manner.

'Now, my lads,' said the captain, 'get an axe and cut away the rigging holding the wreck of that foremast ; we must contrive to make a raft of that lot, and work our way on shore before another blow comes on. I see the mainmast has already broken away, leaving most of the rigging behind.'

All hands went to work with a will, and before nightfall a raft capable of carrying twenty people was put together. As there was every prospect of a calm night, it was resolved to remain on the wreck until morning. A cask of salt pork was fished up, also two more casks of biscuit, and, better than all, two beakers of water.

Next morning the sea was quite smooth, the light wind which blew being off the land, which was unfavourable for making to the islands; but towards noon the wind veered round to the northward, when the captain ordered all hands to leave the ship, after first transferring all the provisions and water obtainable to the raft, also a sail, nautical instruments, a coil of rope, etc. They left the barque which had been their home for many weeks with sad hearts, and, using three oars, endeavoured to work their way towards the nearest island. This, however, they soon found impossible, owing to a strong current setting to the south-west, which carried the raft away at right angles to their proper course. In vain the men tugged at the oars, as island after island was passed, and it soon became apparent that unless the wind changed there was but little chance of reaching the shore. This night was spent in vain attempts to sleep, the raft being allowed to drift where she listed. When day broke, they had worked so far out to sea that no land was visible, and many an anxious glance was cast around in search of a sail, which would be a rare event in those waters, being out of the line of trading ships. The second day and night passed much as the first, with this exception, that the morning sun found the castaways only half a league from a large barque standing under easy sail to the southward. They all cooeed, and waved hats, shirts, and anything likely to attract attention, and soon had the satisfaction of seeing the stranger alter her course and bear down upon them, and in half an hour they were all safely on board the *Independence*, whaler, of Boston, U.S., where they met with every kindness. Eight weeks later they were landed at King George's Sound, and took passage for Melbourne by mail steamer, calling at Adelaide.

We must now return to Tarragal, where we find Mr. Forrester in the midst of another cattle muster, his assistants on this occasion being the brothers Jackson, Myall Sam, and Yardly Mildman; the latter had now become a fair horseman, and was always ready to make himself useful to the squatter. After a hard day's work at branding, the evening found the friends of the family around a cheerful fire in Mrs. Forrester's drawing-room, and the conversation naturally turned upon the subject uppermost in the minds of most of the party, viz., the whereabouts and doings of the young explorers, who were now long overdue.

'It is six months to-day since the *Mohawk* left Port Phillip,' said the squatter, 'and the agents allowed her four months for the voyage. In their last letter, although they were anxious about her, they considered it probable that she might have had consider-able difficulty in getting her cargo, and might also have met with contrary winds. I have written to Lloyds' agent, inquiring whether he has had any intelligence of the barque, and expect an answer by mail to-morrow.'

'If my advice had been taken,' said Mrs. Forrester, 'the boys would never have started on such a wild-goose chase. Should anything happen to my noble boy, I shall never survive it; I have not known a moment's peace since he left me.'

'Oh, mamma!' cried Nellie; 'you must not give way to such morbid fancies, but let us all trust in the Almighty, who watches over all those who travel by land and water. I feel sure that He will permit our dear Edwin and his friends to return to us.'

'I am quite of mamma's opinion,' said Katie, 'and feel something has happened. Oh, what shall I do if my dear brother never returns?' and throwing her arms around her mother, the two mingled their tears, whilst the squatter hastily quitted the room to hide his emotion.

The next day brought a reply from Lloyds' agent, stating that nothing definite had been heard of the *Mohawk*, but that a brig just arrived from Singapore had picked up in the vicinity of the North-west Cape the stern-piece of a ship's long-boat, with the letters **M AWK,** a portion of the timber with other letters having been carried away.

This news Mr. Forrester thought it wise to withhold from the members of his family; therefore he ordered his horse, and rode over to Baylup to consult his friend, Dr. Murray, who he knew was quite as anxious for news as himself. Nellie accompanied her father, having some shopping to attend to in Briar Town.

After the usual greeting, the doctor inquired whether any news had arrived.

'Well, nothing satisfactory,' was the reply; 'but I have a letter from Lloyds' agent which I confess gives me some uneasiness. But read it for yourself.'

Upon perusing the letter, Mr. Murray looked troubled.

'I fear our boys have met with some great misfortune,' was his reply. 'God grant that they may have escaped the perils of the sea! How shall we console their mothers and sisters if they are lost?'

'I dread the thought of it,' replied his friend.

In the meantime Nellie had found her way to Mrs. Murray and Ida, both of whom embraced her warmly. Tears were in the elder lady's eyes as she inquired if they had any news of the missing ones.

'How can we hear from that outlandish part of the world?' exclaimed Ida. 'There seems to be no communication in that direction beyond a place called Swan River.'

'How, indeed!' replied her mother, 'unless we engage a boat specially to go out; but let us hear what papa and Mr. Forrester think about it.'

The result of the conference was that Mr. Murray should write to the Governor of the Swan River Settlement, informing him of the circumstances, and begging that inquiries might be made along the coast for traces of the missing vessel. It would take about six weeks to get a reply from Western Australia, as the only communication was by the English mail-boats calling once a month at King George's Sound, in the southern portion of that colony.

Upon being left to themselves, Nellie and Ida conversed long and earnestly upon the probable fate of the absent ones.

'They would never have thought of such an expedition,' said Ida, 'if you could have given poor Carmel some little encouragement. Poor boy! he loves you very dearly, and I am sure it was your indifference and his dislike of Mr. Mildman's attentions that first caused him to think of this unfortunate exploring trip.'

'Oh, Ida! how can you speak of Mr. Mildman's attentions? You must know that I have never been more than civil to him ; and, dear, I am now sure—that is, I think, that I do like Carmel very much.'

'Oh, you dear'— throwing her arms around Nellie's neck—'I am so glad! but,' with a sigh, 'will the poor boy ever know it ?'

'It is very strange,' quoth Nellie ; 'whilst Carmel was near, although I knew he was devoted to me, I could not realize my own feelings; but now that there is a possibility of never seeing him again, I know that I love him. But what about Edwin, my little inquisitor? Have you no thought beyond your brother for the distant ones ?'

The only reply was a burst of tears from Ida, who threw herself sobbing upon her friend's bosom.

After spending half an hour in vain conjectures, the girls joined their elders at lunch, after which they all adjourned to the veranda, where the gentlemen lit their pipes and settled down for such enjoyment as a myall bowl well filled will afford.

'I see a strange horseman approaching in a hurry,' exclaimed Mr. Murray, 'so I suppose some unfortunate requires my services. No rest for a doctor—in this world, at any rate!' Saying which he walked to the shrubbery-gate to meet the messenger, who handed him a letter, which proved to be from a brother magistrate residing at the seaport town of P——. The letter was as follows:

'P——, October 18, 185—.

'MY DEAR SIR,

'I have received a telegraphic message from Adelaide, stating that your son has just arrived there by mail steamer. From what I can gather, he has been shipwrecked, and picked up at sea with a portion of the crew. It is feared that young Forrester is lost. Break the news to his father, and assure him and Mrs. Forrester of my earnest sympathy in their great trouble.

'I am, very truly yours,

'J. W. ROBERTSON.

'To R. MURRAY, ESQ., Briar Town.'

The feeling of gladness which Mr. Murray experienced in reading the first few lines gave place to grief at the loss of his young friend. He read the note twice through before speaking, and then directed the messenger to put his horse in the stable and wait for a reply.

'Well,' inquired the squatter, 'is it an urgent call? Is there anyone ill?'

'Not exactly,' was the reply; 'but as it concerns my wife, I must consult her on the subject, if you will excuse me for a few moments.'

So saying, husband and wife withdrew to the parlour, where the doctor first broke the news of Carmel's safety. I need not describe the joy of the good lady at hearing such good news, and she was about to call Ida and Nellie to share her pleasure, when she was stopped by her husband, who read the part of his letter referring to Edwin.

'Oh, my dear boy! How shall we break the news to them all? But perhaps it may not be true; we must make the best of it, and wait for Carmel's return.'

It was then arranged that Mr. Murray

should inform the squatter of the contents of his letter, whilst Mrs. Murray undertook to break the news to the girls.

In the afternoon Mr. Forrester and Nellie set out with saddened hearts upon their return to Tarragal, which at once became a house of mourning. To Mrs. Forrester and Nellie the days which elapsed before Carmel's arrival were got through with quiet expectation, hoping against hope. Neither would permit herself to believe that she had seen the last of the noble son and brother. On the other hand, the bereaved father and mother gave way to their grief, the former accusing himself for want of firmness in allowing his boy to leave home.

Upon reaching Melbourne, Carmel lost no time in procuring horses for himself, Dick, and Balgarra, as the homeward journey had to be performed on horseback. As they neared Briar Town the whole population turned out to welcome Carmel, and it was noticed that almost every man wore a crape band on the left arm, out of respect for their lost favourite.

CHAPTER XV.

GLAD TIDINGS.

THE Tarragal people were amongst the first visitors to arrive, and Carmel had to recount again and again every incident connected with the wreck, also their explorations on shore, dwelling repeatedly on Edwin's tact and bravery in saving him from the natives when wounded. The recital was very gratifying to the grief-stricken parents and sisters, whilst Ida became quite hysterical at the mention of Edwin's name, much to the alarm of her mother, whose eyes were only just opened to the fact that her daughter's affections were touched.

Notwithstanding the favourable accounts brought by Carmel of the new country, his father and Mr. Forrester decided to have nothing more to do with it. However,

Carmel published the report of the expedition, giving an account of the country and his opinion as to its value for grazing purposes. From the nugget found by Balgarra he had a mourning ring made, with the initials **E. F.** thereon.

Shortly after his return he purchased a large tract of country in the Tatiara—a district that was now attracting some attention—and moving up to his runs he secured two thousand ewes and commenced sheep farming, with varying success at first; but after awhile, as the country around him became stocked, his prospects improved, upon which he wrote a formal proposal to Nellie, to which that young lady gave a favourable reply, but stated that she would not become engaged until a year had expired since her brother's death; and with this reply Carmel was obliged to be content. Yardly Mildman, although not in affluent circumstances, also contemplated matrimony, judging by his attentions to Ida; but that young lady treated his attentions most coolly, so that he could not screw his courage up to proposing form.

Nearly a year had now elapsed since the wreck of the *Mohawk*, and our friends at Tarragal, although they had not forgotten their darling Edwin, were to some extent reconciled to his loss. It would be no hard matter to follow the squatter's thoughts, as he sat for hours of an evening in the veranda smoking his pipe.

On one of these occasions he was roused from his reverie by the barking of dogs, indicating the arrival of a stranger, and in a few minutes our old acquaintance, Lieutenant Thomson, rode up and dismounted at the door.

'Well, this is a surprise,' said the squatter, wringing his hands. 'Come in, Mrs. Forrester and the girls will be so glad to see you.'

The ladies were indeed pleased to see the young officer, who was a great favourite with them all.

'Have you ridden out alone?' he was asked.

'I have a friend with me, but he loitered on the road, and being anxious to see you, I pushed on. The *Emu* only arrived yesterday morning in port, and she sails again to-morrow night, so that I have only two days' leave. Indeed, we should not have called in at your port at all, but had special reasons for doing so.'

' Well,' said Mr. Forrester, ' we are grateful to those special reasons for giving us the pleasure of your company, although we cannot offer you much in the way of amusement. Tarragal is not what it used to be; we have had a great misfortune since you left us.'

' So I have heard. But perhaps it is not so bad as you expect; your son may still return.' A shake of the head was the only reply. ' Well,' said Thomson, ' I have heard some news which leads me to hope that Edwin still lives, and is now on his way home; and it is to consult you on this subject that I am here.'

' Oh, my darling boy lives!' cried Mrs. Forrester. ' You know something or you would not give me this hope.'

The whole party were now clustered around the young officer, imploring him to put them out of suspense.

'Very well, then, you may hope for the best. Your boy will shortly be with you; in fact, he is my companion, and is now only waiting my call in that clump of wattles.'

In answer to a cooee, the gallop of a horse was heard, and in a few moments a young man, well browned and bearded, had thrown himself from his horse, and was clasped in his mother's arms. Here we will leave him for the present.

To explain the appearance of our hero, we must refer to the night of the wreck, when we saw him along with two sailors swept off the *Mohawk's* deck. When he found himself clear of the barque, and realized his position, the instinct of self-preservation induced him to strike out and endeavour to keep his head above water as long as possible, but in the seething foam with which he was environed this was no easy matter. But now fortune befriended him in the shape of the broken main-mast, which he struck against and at once grasped, and with this support he was carried shorewards slowly but surely, and shortly after sunrise was enabled to land on the

14

sandy beach of a low island. The exhausted youth had great difficulty in wading his way through the surf, but at last reached *terra firma,* when his first act was to fall on his knees and offer up thanks for his miraculous escape from a watery grave, after which he mounted a mound of sand and cast his eyes seawards in search of the wreck, but could make out nothing, except the raging billows still rolling in with great force.

As the sun came forth, Edwin first wrung out his clothes, ran along the beach until he had produced a little warmth in his chilled limbs, and then started in quest of food of some sort; but for some time he was unsuccessful, a few planks, a portion of a boat, and some cordage being all that he could find along the western shore. On the eastern shore, however, he was more fortunate, as he came upon thousands of sea-fowl of various descriptions, and found eggs in hundreds, many of which were quite fresh. Young birds unable to fly were also plentiful, so that he had now no fear of dying from starvation; the only trouble was to get a fire, but in the meantime he ate

some raw eggs; then, remembering having
seen Balgarra light a fire by friction, he
searched about until he came upon some
suitable twigs. Selecting a straight round
piece about eighteen inches long, he rounded
off the end; then, taking a piece slightly
larger, he made a shallow hole in the centre.
Putting the latter on the ground in a
horizontal position, he held the light piece
perpendicularly between the palms of both
hands, with the rounded end resting in the
hollow of the lower piece; then, rubbing
his hands with a downward pressure, he soon
brought smoke out of the wood. But smoke
does not always indicate fire, and at last he
ceased his exertions, and, after a rest, went
at it again, this time putting a little sand in
the hollow of the wood. This plan had the
desired effect, and in less than three minutes
he saw sparks amongst the powdered wood,
and very soon contrived to ignite some dry
grass and kindle a fire, after which he
prepared dinner of roast chicken, with eggs
cooked in like manner.

His next anxiety was water, as up to the
present time he had only found a few gallons

14—2

in hollow rocks; but this he knew would soon be exhausted without another fall of rain to replenish it. In continuing his search along the southern shore he came upon some more wreckage, also a cask of beef; the latter he rolled up on the sand and covered with seaweed, then continued his search for water, but only succeeded in discovering two more small rock-holes.

To the north-east of Edwin's territory, three-quarters of a mile distant, was another low island, which our hero determined to reach, in hopes of finding a better supply of water; he therefore collected such wreckage as seemed most suitable, and constructed a light raft, which he guided round to the eastern side of his island by wading through the surf. Taking advantage of the sea breeze, which usually set in every afternoon, he worked his raft well up to windward, and started on his voyage of discovery, taking a long pole with which to guide his frail craft. The channel, with the exception of about 200 yards in the centre, proved to be very shallow, so that he could pole along without difficulty, and at the end of two hours he landed on the opposite shore, and secured his raft, after which he had a look round and prepared a camp for the night.

Next morning saw our hero early astir, and he found that this island contained a quantity of grass and other vegetation, and, better than all, he came upon fresh wallaby tracks, which he followed to where they formed a beaten path, leading to a sandy hollow; here the marsupials had excavated a hole about two feet deep, in which was about a gallon of spring-water. Our hero tasted the water, and gave vent to a shout of joy; he now knew that he could exist for months on these islands upon wallaby, fish, eggs, etc. To get back to his first refuge he had only to take advantage of the land wind, which blew early in the morning, whilst the sea breeze would bring him back in the evening to the eastern island, where he resolved to make his head-quarters until some passing ship should pick him up.

He now built himself a hut with bushes and grass, after the style of a native's gunyah; afterwards he constructed a wallaby-trap, which was prepared in this way: A close

fence of stakes and bushes was erected in a
circle round the spring, openings being left
on the beaten paths ; inside each of the gaps
a hole was sunk about five feet deep and
two feet in diameter, which was then covered
with light twigs and grass, with a top
layer of sand, and the trap was complete.
The unsuspecting wallaby would come
hopping along the path, when his weight
would break through the flimsy covering and
he was secure. Scarcely a morning passed
without getting two or more in this way, the
haunches of which, roasted with a thin slice
of salt beef, were most palatable. The skins
were dried in the sun, and afterwards stitched
together with sinews, taken from the tail,
thus making a nice warm rug, which Edwin
stood in great need of.

Two months had now passed away; still
no sail hove in sight, and our hero began to
feel a veritable Robinson Crusoe. He often
wondered how it fared with his companions ;
he knew by the wreckage washed ashore
from time to time that the vessel had broken
up, but he hoped that a boat had been saved
upon which the crew might be enabled to

reach the mainland, from whence they would no doubt contrive to reach some of the out-lying sheep-stations in Western Australia.

Bush-fires could be seen almost daily on the mainland, but these Edwin concluded were caused by natives, and this thought, with the uncertainty of the treatment he might expect from the blacks, deterred him from making any attempt to gain the main-land, although he was most anxious to get away, knowing the great grief of his parents and sisters at the uncertainty of his fate. Ida also was seldom absent from his thoughts.

Freshwater Island, as Edwin named his home, was composed of a series of sand-ridges, portions of which were bare of vege-tation, and this loose sand was continually moved by the strong south-east winds which prevail in summer along this coast, in some cases rifts being blown clean through the ridges, leaving the surface of the ground bare, and in many instances with a hard, even surface of black sand. On passing through one of these gaps, Edwin's attention was attracted by a very rusty piece of hoop-iron, the end of which projected out of the ground; he took hold of the iron with the intention of pulling it up, but found it resisted his endeavours.

Now, there is nothing in an ordinary piece of rusty hoop-iron to attract attention, and, no doubt, had Edwin seen it anywhere else, he would not have given it a second thought; but now a spirit of curiosity impelled him to have it out. Therefore, he procured a pointed stick, and digging down a few inches, struck a substance harder than sand, and putting down his hand, he picked up two foreign-looking gold coins.

For a few moments surprise held him speechless, then a light suddenly broke upon him. He remembered the captain's tale of Houtman's Abrolhos, and that treasure had been secreted there by Dutch mutineers. He now concluded that his island formed one of that group, and that his lucky star had led him to the spot where the treasure lay hidden.

Taking his stick, he again dug into the sand, and in half an hour had unearthed more gold than he could carry, the strong iron-bound boxes containing the gold having completely decayed, leaving only some highly-corroded iron clamps.

The sudden acquisition of wealth is, no doubt, a very agreeable sensation, but in Edwin's case the pleasure was somewhat marred by the inability to use his riches. He would freely have given the whole for a passage in some ship to Melbourne. However, to be prepared for an emergency, he next morning started for his first island, and brought over the beef-cask, which he emptied of its contents, and putting some grass in the bottom, packed away the gold, putting alternate layers of grass to prevent jingling and to fill up space; when about six inches from the top, he filled the remaining space with cowries and other shells, which he had collected from time to time. When all was ready, he placed the head in the cask as neatly as possible, and drove the hoops down with a stone, after which he covered the cask over with bushes and sand to keep the sun off.

The lucky find made our hero more than ever anxious to get away from the islands; but for many months he looked in vain for a sail, and had almost decided upon trying to reach the mainland on the raft, when one afternoon he made out a ship to the westward heading up for the islands. At first he would not permit himself to believe that he would be rescued, fearing that the vessel would pass on her way without nearing the shore. His delight may therefore be better imagined than described when he saw her head up to his first island, which he had named ' Mohawk,' and when two miles from shore drop anchor.

When Edwin first saw the vessel he lit a fire, which he kept well supplied with green fuel, to cause a black smoke ; he therefore thought that his fire was the cause of the ship's coming to anchor. Had the wind been off the land he would have put to sea at once in the raft ; but, under the circumstances, he was obliged to wait until morning, unless a boat should come round to him.

When he arose next morning, his first move was to cast his eyes in the direction of the vessel. A fear was upon him that she might have cleared out again ; but no, the vessel was still at anchor, and as the land-breeze was now on, he was quickly on board his raft and working his way across to Mohawk Island.   He carried some fire over, and soon had a blaze on the highest hillock. The fire was seen from the ship, and a flag run up to the peak in reply.

Half an hour afterwards a boat left the ship's side, impelled by four strong rowers, who soon reached the shore, when the officer in charge leaped to land and accosted our hero, who stood on the beach, his hair unkempt and clothing in tatters, a small wallaby rug being the only covering on his shoulders.

'Good morning, young man. Are you a castaway? You seem in a sorry plight!' said the officer, whom Edwin recognised as Lieutenant Thomson, of H.M.S. *Emu.*

CHAPTER XVI.

HOME AT LAST.

FOR a few moments Edwin was unable to speak, so excited was he at the prospect of deliverance, but, recovering himself, he held out his hand, saying:

'I see, lieutenant, you do not recognise me, but that is quite excusable. Yes, I am a castaway, and had begun to fear that I should never leave these islands; but now, thank God! I shall see my friends again.'

'In Heaven's name!' cried the officer, 'who are you? I seem to know the voice, but cannot recognise the features.'

'Don't you remember Tarragal and Edwin Forrester?' was the reply.

The young officer leaped towards him and wrung his hand warmly, saying:

'I thought you were drowned. We called

at King George's Sound on our way round, and heard of the loss of the *Mohawk* and of your certain death. How fortunate it is that we were instructed to visit and verify the position of these islands on our way up the coast, where our special mission is to inspect and fix the position of Ritchie's Reef, which is said to be incorrectly laid down on the Admiralty charts. But come on board; I must rig you out and introduce you to the captain, who will be very glad to see you.'

The captain and officers were all most kind to the castaway, who soon became a great favourite. When he had recounted his adventures and fortunate escapes, he was advised to write a book. He, however, said nothing about the discovery of the hidden treasure, but informed the lieutenant that he had some things on shore that he would like to bring away, including a cask of curios, which he valued highly.

' Oh, very well ; we shall be here all day, as we have to take morning and evening sights for longitude, so that I shall have lots of time to send a boat's crew with you to bring away your property.'

The cask was brought safely on board, and next morning sail was made, and a course shaped for the North-west Cape and the Reef. After fixing the latter, and doing other survey work, they cleared away for Port Phillip (calling *en route* at P——), where they dropped anchor, six weeks after leaving Mohawk Island.

Edwin's first step upon landing was to get his cask of curios on shore, and the contents lodged in the Union Bank; after which he started with his friend Thomson for Tarragal, where they arrived, as we have seen, the next afternoon.

After the first happy greetings were over, tea was announced; and then Edwin had to recount every incident that befel him from the moment of being washed off the wreck up to the time he was picked up by the *Emu*, the one topic upon which he was reticent being the discovery of the treasure on the Abrolhos; this he intended for a pleasant sequel to his tale.

'We are very thoughtless,' said Mr. Forrester, 'not to have remembered our friends at Baylup. I will send off a messenger at once with the welcome news—they will all be as much rejoiced as ourselves.'

'Thanks, father,' said Edwin; 'I was about to request that you would do so. From inquiries made *en route* I hear that they are all well, with the exception of Ida.'

'Yes, my dear,' replied his mother. 'Dear Ida has not been herself for many months, but I trust that your return will cheer her up; I must ask her over for a week or two.'

'Let us all go over to-morrow, and call upon them,' suggested our hero. 'Your messenger can inform them of our intention. I can ride with the girls whilst Pater and Mater can drive the phaeton. I long to mount Douglas again. I presume the old fellow is all right?'

'Yes, my boy, he is fresh and well,' said his father; 'in fact I think you will find him too fresh—I would not have him ridden during your absence.'

I need not describe the delight of the Baylup party at receiving the glad tidings, although at first they got a severe fright, owing to Ida having swooned; however, joy seldom kills, and the next few days were happy ones with the two families. Carmel had been written to and was shortly expected.

Edwin now made known his good fortune, and it was arranged that the whole party should take a holiday trip to town, and see the wonderful find.

The gold coin was valued by the bank-manager at £40,000, and he congratulated our hero upon his good fortune.

Six months have now passed away since our hero's return, and Briar Town is once more very gay. Impromptu flag-poles have been erected at intervals along the main street, upon which bunting in great variety is displayed.

The reason of this unusual display is a double-wedding—as the lawyers would say, Edwin and Ida on the one part, with Carmel and Nellie on the other part. Balgarra was in great glee: he appeared in the height of fashion, displaying any amount of white satin ribbon in his button-hole, and his black face was lit up with joy.

After the ceremony, the wedding-party

adjourned to Mr. Murray's hospitable mansion, where a sumptuous breakfast was prepared. In the afternoon the happy couples departed, Carmel with his bride to his home in the north, whilst Edwin took his wife to a beautiful home on the Mount Elephant Plains, where he had purchased a sheep station some weeks before.

Yardly Mildman was induced to try his fortunes at sheep-farming, and with Carmel's assistance he secured a piece of country adjoining the former, where in course of time he made a competence.

The last I heard of Dick Evans was on the evening of the double wedding, when he was seen lying flat on the sward, face downwards, striking out with legs and arms, in the vain attempt to reach his hat, which had fallen some six feet away. An old chum walking by accosted him with :

' Well, Dick, old man, what's the trouble?'

' Why, look here,' said Dick, without ceasing his struggles, ' I have fallen into the river, and am swimming after my hat, but can't get up to the darned thing!'

His companion fairly roared with laughter.

15

'Why, man, you are not in the water! Don't you see I am walking upright?'

'Well, I'm blowed!' was the reply. 'Why, I must be drunk!'—which assertion his friend did not venture to dispute.

The younger members of our story still live, and are as happy as it is possible to be in this world of care. Edwin and Carmel are both ranked amongst the wool-kings of Victoria, and may be seen on the stand at Flemington on Cup Day, whilst Ida and Nellie are to be found amongst the gaily and richly-dressed ladies who on that day throng the Lawn, and here in the midst of enjoyment we will leave them.

THE END.

BILLING AND SONS, PRINTERS, GUILDFORD.

Publications

of

Messrs. GAY and BIRD

22, BEDFORD STREET, STRAND,

LONDON

IMPORTERS OF AMERICAN BOOKS

Special Agents for the Sale of the Publications

HOUGHTON, MIFFLIN & Co., BOSTON, U.S.A.

LONDON PUBLISHERS OF

THE ATLANTIC MONTHLY. Price 1s. Net. Subscription 15s.
THE NEW WORLD. Price 3s. Net. Subscription 13s.
THE METAPHYSICAL MAGAZINE. Price 1s. 6d. Net. Subscription 14s
THE NEW SCIENCE REVIEW. Price 2s. Net. Subscription 9s.

ALL POST FREE

GAY & BIRD'S PUBLICATIONS.

TIMOTHY'S QUEST. By Kate Douglas Wiggin. Popular Edition. *Fifteenth.* Crown 8vo., tastefully bound, 2s. 6d.

> *The Times* :—"By this felicitous sketch Mrs. Wiggin has firmly established her literary reputation."

> *Punch* :—"In the arid life of the book-reviewer there is sometimes found the oasis of opportunity to recommend a book worth reading. My Baronite has by chance come upon such an one in '*Timothy's Quest*' by Kate Douglas Wiggin. . . . . The book is an almost perfect idyl. . . . . It is the best thing of the kind that has reached us from America since '*Little Lord Fauntleroy*' crossed the Atlantic."

> *Queen* :—"It is surely '*David Copperfield*' over again."

> *Scottish Leader* :—"One of the prettiest and most charming stories recently issued. . . . . Sure to obtain an honourable and permanent place in literature."

A CATHEDRAL COURTSHIP AND PENELOPE'S EXPE-RIENCES. By Kate Douglas Wiggin. Popular Edition. *Sixth.* Crown 8vo., illustrated and tastefully bound in cloth gilt, 2s. 6d.

> *Saturday Review* :—"A charming book."

> *Daily News* :—"Both stories are idylls. . . . From the first to the last the volume is full of life, humour and colour."

> *Manchester Courier* :—"Amusing in the extreme, ... perfectly delicious."

> *Punch* :—"There is only one word that will fittingly describe 'A Cathedral Courtship.' It is delightful."

> *Scotsman* :—"The book is in every way delightful."

THE VILLAGE WATCH-TOWER. By Kate Douglas Wiggin.

Second Edition. Crown 8vo., cloth, 3s. 6d.

Mr. W. L. Courtney in reviewing this book in the DAILY TELEGRAPH, *says:—*
"Anyone who has read 'Timothy's Quest' will know what to expect
from Mrs. Wiggin—something half-way between tears and laughter,
humour and pathos ; the tragi-comedy of simple human lives, possessing, whatever else they may be devoid of, an undeniable charm. . . .
It is the extraordinarily acute perception, the happiness of phrase, the
naturalness of the manner which constitute the charm of 'The Village
Watch-Tower'—as well as the absence of anything artificial or laboured,
the justness and appropriateness of the strokes with which the portraits are completed. Mrs. Wiggin has a keen sense of fun, but it is of
the quiet meditative sort, which comes nearer to humour, and realises
what, after Virgil, we call 'the sense of tears in human things.' . . . .
It is the exquisite felicity of the whole which strikes the reader, hardly
a word too much, not a colour or a pencil-stroke amiss."

Daily News :—" Every little story is the work of an artist, who can make the
joys and sorrows she depicts the reader's own for the time being."

North British Daily Mail :—" We have nothing but the most unqualified praise
to bestow upon this book. It has the scent of pine forests and new-
mown hay in all its stories."

Christian World :—" Mrs. Wiggin is to be congratulated on this collection of
short stories. The book is a mine of character, of amusement and
pathos."

Sun :—" Pathos and humour pass and repass into one another without let or
hindrance ; each story is complete and polished. Better workmanship
it were impossible to ask ; and Mrs. Wiggin's art is doubly happy in
concealing itself, without a shadow of affectation or of conscious arti-
fice. And this is the height of art. . . . Never before, I think, has she
ventured in waters so deep ; never before has she succeeded more
absolutely. The book is a little masterpiece. . . . It is a book that is
safe to become a general favourite."

Leeds Mercury :—" These six stories are remarkable. No one is the least likely
to put down such a volume unread, for the appeal to sympathy is
manifold, and lies half-way between laughter and tears."

Manchester Guardian :—" 'The Village Watch-Tower' is a collection of charming sketches of American village life, told with all the humour and
delicate sentiment we have come to expect from Mrs. Wiggin."

Scotsman :—" The stories are all written with the charm of narrative that have
made its writer's books so popular both here and in America."

Literary World :—" We have read it three times with growing admiration. '

THE BIRDS' CHRISTMAS CAROL. By Kate Douglas Wiggin. Impl. 16mo., eight illustrations, cloth back, 1s. 6d.

THE STORY OF PATSY. By Kate Douglas Wiggin. Impl. 16mo., eleven illustrations, cloth back, 1s. 6d.

THE STORY HOUR. A Book for Home and Kindergarten. By Kate Douglas Wiggin and her sister Nora A. Smith. Crown 8vo., illustrated, cloth, 2s. 6d.

A SUMMER IN A CAÑON. A Californian Story. By Kate Douglas Wiggin. Crown 8vo., illustrated, cloth, 3s. 6d.

Scotsman :—" The work is a fresh and charming tale of country life in California, full of good spirits and healthy thoughts."

POLLY OLIVER'S PROBLEM. A Story for Girls. By Kate Douglas Wiggin. Third Edition. Crown 8vo., with eight Illustrations, cloth gilt, 3s. 6d.

Daily Telegraph —" In none of Mrs. Wiggin's felicitous stories is the charm of unaffected freshness and spontaneous geniality more prevailingly potent, than in her last character sketch ' Polly Oliver's Problem'."

Scotsman :—" It is a delightful story."

Glasgow Herald :—" This is an admirably-written and thoroughly interesting story for girls."

Scottish Leader :—" No page will be skipped, surely Louisa Alcott has at last found a successor.'

Dundee Advertiser :—" A delightful story for girls."

CHILDREN'S RIGHTS. By Kate Douglas Wiggin, and her Sister NORA A. SMITH, with a Preface by EMILY A. E. SHIRREFF (President of the London Frœbel Society). Third Edition. Crown 8vo., cloth, ornamental, 5s.

Athenæum :—" We strongly recommend this volume to parents and to all who have to do with the bringing up of children."

Educational Times :—" We thank Mrs. Wiggin most heartily for her little book which we have thoroughly enjoyed."

THE REPUBLIC OF CHILDHOOD. Vol. I. Frœbel's Gifts.
By Kate Douglas Wiggin and her sister Nora Archibald Smith.
Crown 8vo., cloth, 5s.

Scotsman :—" It is, as its authors define it, a popular treatise on a scientific subject ; and young teachers who have recognised the greatness of the Kindergarten idea, and young mothers who wish help in the education of their children from a knowledge of what the Kindergarten idea really is, will both find it well worth reading."

Daily Chronicle :—" The rationale of each gift, and their co-relation, are clearly explained and illustrated by the authors, and numerous hints are given for varied exercises and subsidiary uses to which they may be put."

Liverpool Post :—" Those who essay this method of instruction will find valuable assistance in ' Frœbel's Gifts.' "

Manchester Guardian :—"The system is set forth in its scientific gradations and the development of the rational faculty in children is very thoughtfully discussed."

MELODY. The Story of a Child. By Laura E. Richards.
Imperial 16mo., cloth, 2s. 6d.

Schoolmaster :—" This is a beautifully written little sketch of a blind child's life. There is infinite pathos in the way the subject is treated, and the word painting is most exquisite and graphic. The book is very tastefully bound, and would not be out of place in the best library."

Newcastle Chronicle :—"The story is told with considerable power and pathos."

Bookseller :—" It is a long time since we have read anything quite so charming and delightful . . . it is throughout written with such insight imagination, and pathos, that the critic has nothing to say save that the whole is so perfect, that any alteration or change must needs be for the worse."

Lady's Pictorial :—" A very pretty and pathetic story."

Church Times :—" A perfectly delightful little story . . . . which can be enjoyed alike by children and by children of a larger growth."

MORELLI DOMENICO. A Sketch of the Life and Work of the
Painter. By Ashton R. Willard. With eight Heliotypes. Small 4to., cloth, 5s. net.

AMERICAN WRITERS OF TO-DAY. By Henry C. Vedder.
Crown 8vo., cloth, gilt top, 7s. 6d.

6

Great Captains Series:

ALEXANDER. A History of the Origin and Growth of the Art of War, from the Earliest Times to the Battle of Ipsus, B.C. 301; with a detailed account of the Campaigns of the great Macedonian. With 237 Charts, Maps, Plans of Battles and Tactical Manœuvres, Cuts of Armour, Uniforms, Siege Devices, and Portraits. 8vo., cloth, 20s. net.

HANNIBAL. A History of the Art of War among the Carthagenians and Romans, down to the Battle of Pydna, 168 B.C.; with a detailed account of the Second Tunic War. With 227 Charts, Maps, Plans of Battles and Tactical Manœuvres, Cuts of Armour, Weapons and Uniforms. 8vo., cloth, 20s. net.

CÆSAR. A History of the Art of War among the Romans from the Second Tunic War down to the Fall of the Roman Empire; with a detailed account of the Gallic and Civil Wars. With 275 Charts, Maps, Plans of Battles and Tactical Manœuvres, etc. 8vo, cloth, 20s. net.

GUSTAVUS ADOLPHUS. A History of the Art of War from the revival after the Middle Ages to the end of the Spanish Succession War; with a detailed account of the Campaigns of the great Swede, and the most famous Campaigns of Turenne, Conde, Eugene and Marlborough. With 234 Charts, Maps, Plans of Battles, and Tactical Manœuvres, and Cuts of Uniforms and Weapons. Two volumes in one, 8vo., cloth, 20s. net.

ELECTRICITY FOR EVERYBODY: Its Nature and Uses Explained. By Philip Atkinson, M.A., PL.D. Crown 8vo., 100 illustrations, cloth, 5s.

> CONTENTS:— Chapter I. The Nature of Electricity and Electric Transmission.—II. Static Electricity.—III. Electric Batteries.—IV. Magnetism.—V. Dynamos.—VI. Electric Motors.—VII. Electric Lighting.—VIII. Heat and Electricity.—IX. The Telegraph and Telephone.
>
> *Scotsman:*—"There are many books of its kind; but few more likely to suit the requirements of readers not specially or professionally concerned with its subject."
>
> *Daily News:*—"Is a sensible-written manual for the instruction of those possessing little or no technical knowledge of a subject of ever-growing importance."

DOCTRINE AND LIFE. A Study of some of the Principal Truths of the Christian Religion in the Relation to Christian Experience. By George B. Stevens, Ph.D., D.D. Crown 8vo., cloth, 6s. 6d.

7

THE AUTOCRAT OF THE BREAKFAST TABLE. By Oliver
Wendell Holmes. Two vols., crown 8vo. Fifteen beautiful photogravures and many engraved text illustrations by Howard Pyle. Printed in the most careful manner, and bound in the most attractive style. Cloth gilt, gilt top, with slip cloth wrappers, 21s.

LARGE PAPER EDITION, limited to thirty copies for this country. Handsomely bound in full vellum, with India proofs of plates, Four Guineas nett.

The Baron de Book-Worms in PUNCH :—" Many thanks for these two handsome volumes, for among all books these be most welcome to the constant lover of old literary friends."

Glasgow Herald :—" No finer edition could be wished for."

DOROTHY Q. By Oliver Wendell Holmes. Together
with "A Ballad of a Boston Tea Party," and "Grandmother's Story of Bunker Hill Battle." One volume. Crown 8vo., 62 illustrations and many beautiful borders, head and tail pieces, by Howard Pyle. Bound in grey cloth with quaint letterings and ornaments in silver. 5s. net.

Times :—"A copiously and charmingly illustrated edition."

Publishers' Circular :—" One of the prettiest illustrated books of the season."

Daily Graphic :—"A dainty gift book. . . . must be seen to be appreciated."

THE ONE-HOSS SHAY. By Oliver Wendell Holmes.
With its Companion Poems "HOW THE OLD HORSE WON THE BET," and "THE BROOMSTICK TRAIN." Crown 8vo., 62 spirited Illustrations by Howard Pyle, quaintly bound in rough calf, 6s. net.

Spectator :—" Most appropriately illustrated."

Glasgow Herald.—"His illustrations are a source of great delight."

Truth :—" Exquisitely got-up and illustrated edition."

THE OLIVER WENDELL HOLMES YEAR BOOK. With a
charming new Portrait of O. W. Holmes, at the age of 84. 12mo, attractively bound, 3s. 6d.

This dainty book consists of admirable passages carefully selected from the prose and poetry of Dr. Holmes, for every day of the year. His marvellous good sense, wisdom, and wit are conspicuous on every page, and make the Year-book a fit and charming souvenir of the delightful "Autocrat."

IN THE DOZY HOURS. By Agnes Repplier. Crown 8vo., cloth, gilt top, 5s.

Athenæum:—"The only fault we have to find with Miss Repplier's delightful little volume of Essays 'In the Dozy Hours' is that some of them are too short. . . . With this small reservation we have nothing but praise for this book."

Saturday Review:—"Miss Repplier's claims to be accounted of the true succession (of English Essayists)—Augustan, Georgian, Victorian—are incontestible. She has a fine critical faculty, and is mistress of a charming style. She has wit, a fund of good sense, and humour—English 'humour' and American 'humor.' . . . But there is not one of these essays that is not marked by rare sanity of judgment, an invigorating tone, and the inspiring grace of humour."

ESSAYS IN IDLENESS. By Agnes Repplier. Second Edition. Crown 8vo., cloth, gilt top, 5s.

Mr. Le Gallienne in the Star:—"Of their kind, a very entertaining kind, no one just now is writing better essays than Miss Repplier."

BOOKS AND MEN. By Agnes Repplier. Crown 8vo., cloth, gilt top, 5s

ESSAYS IN MINIATURE. By Agnes Repplier. Second Edition. Crown 8vo., cloth, gilt top, 5s.

Saturday Review :—"Some of those rare hours of placid and genuine enjoyment is in store for the readers of 'Essays in Miniature.'"

Review of Reviews :—"Miss Repplier is almost as entertaining an essayist as Mr. Andrew Lng."

POINTS OF VIEW. By Agnes Repplier. Third Edition. Crown 8vo., cloth, gilt top, 5s.

Glasgow Herald:—"Those in want of a genuine literary treat cannot do better than go to 'Points of View.'"

SYNONYMS AND AUTONYMS. A Complete Dictionary of Synonyms and words of opposite meaning. By The Rt. Rev. Samuel Fallows. With an Appendix embracing a Dictionary of Briticisms, Americanisms, Colloquial Phrases, etc., in current use; the Grammatical Uses of Prepositions and Prepositions Discriminated ; a List of Homonyms and Homophonous Words a Collection of Foreign Phrases, and a complete list of Abbreviations and Contractions used in Writing and Printing. Crown 8vo., 512 pp., cloth, 3s. 6d.

WALT WHITMAN. Leaves of Grass. Being his Complete
Poems. Demy 8vo., portrait, cloth, gilt top, 9s.

——————————— **Complete Prose Works.** Portrait,
Uniform with the above. 9s.

THE VISION OF SIR LAUNFAL. By James Russell Lowell.
Crown 8vo., 8 charming Photogravures by E. H. Garrett and Portrait of
Lowell in 1842, with long curls and deep linen collar, tastefully bound.
6s. nett.

Punch :—"A dainty book indeed."

Spectator :—"Nothing is so interesting as the portrait. . . . . A very poetical
head indeed."

N.B.—Portrait on India Paper, 12 by 9, 2s. nett.

A FABLE FOR CRITICS. By James Russell Lowell.
Crown 8vo., cloth 5s.

. An Edition for the Book-lover, with 26 outline Portraits of the Authors
mentioned in the poem, and a Facsimile in Colour of the Rhyming Title-Page of
the First Edition.

JAPANESE GIRLS AND WOMEN. By Alice Mabel Bacon.
Third Edition. Crown 8vo., cloth, gilt top, 5s.

Daily Telegraph :—"The chapters she has penned are delightful. . .   Her
book ought to be popular and well read for a long time to come."

Queen:—"There are pages, nay, whole chapters, of the book that simply
charm. . . . . I hope to find space for a fuller account of a book
which I have read with quite unusual interest and pleasure."

Morning Post :—"The book not only treats of much that has not before been
generally known but is written in a pleasing style."

A JAPANESE INTERIOR. By Alice Mabel Bacon. Crown
8vo., cloth, gilt top, 5s.

Glasgow Herald :—"Most enjoyable reading."

Sun :—"It is a perfectly charming study, written easily and gracefully, and
giving an insight into Japanese life such as many more hundred pages
of dull statistics could never afford their reader. The descriptions
are vivid, brilliant, finished, and the whole work is thoroughly
entertaining."

JERUSALEM ILLUSTRATED. By G. Robinson Lees,
F.R.G.S., Author of "Bible Scenes from the Holy Land.' With a
preface by The Right Rev. Bishop Blyth, of Jerusalem and an
appendix illustrating the models of Herr Baurath von Schick Ritter,
with descriptive letterpress translated by the Rev. J. E. Hanauer.
Demy 8vo., copiously illustrated from negatives taken by the Author
during a residence of several years in Jerusalem. Cloth gilt, 6s.

A PURITAN PAGAN. By Julien Gordon. Author of "A
Diplomat's Diary," "Mdle. Reseda," "Marionettes," etc. Crown 8vo.,
cloth extra, 5s.

> *Morning Post:*—"A graceful and original heroine, and her experiences are
> extremely varied."

> *Sun :*—"A novel that should be a great success."

> *Daily Telegraph :*—"An ingenious and eventful story of 'a man's sin and
> repentance' . . . . brightly written throughout, and abounds in
> clever word-sketches of American character and social observances."

EROTICA. By Arthur Clark Kennedy. Fcap. 8vo., frontispiece, cloth extra, 3s. 6d. net.

> *Scotsman :*—"Shows considerable accomplishment in the art of making sweet
> verses."

ADRIATICA. By Percy Pinkerton. Fcap. 8vo., frontispiece,
cloth extra, 5s. net.

> A charming Volume of Poems, chiefly about Venice, with an Original Poem by
> J. ADDINGTON SYMONDS to the Author. Edition limited to 250 copies.

SIDNEY LANIER'S POEMS. Edited by his Wife. With
a Memorial by William Hayes Ward. 8vo., Portrait, tastefully
bound in cloth gilt, gilt top, 7s. 6d. net.

> *Spectator :*—"We have in Lanier an original poet—one more original, we
> think, than the United States has ever yet produced; more original
> than any poet whom England has produced during the last thirty years
> at least."

> *Review of Reviews :*—"Than the short series, 'Hymns of the Marshes,' we
> know of nothing in any poetry more beautiful or more quivering with
> the spirit of nature."

THE DELMONICO COOK BOOK. How to Buy Food, how to Cook It, and how to Serve It. By Alessandro Filippini,
(for 25 years Chef at Delmonico's, New York). Large 8vo., new and revised edition, strongly bound in white American cloth, 12s. net

This work is designed not only for Clubs, Hotels and Restaurants, but more especially for Private Families. In it will be found Menus for Breakfast, Luncheon and Dinner for every day in the year, beside Menus for Celebrated Dinners which have been given at Delmonico's from time to time.

Queen :—" A book which is sure to find its way to any kitchen ruled by a cook worthy of the name."

Field :—" We can strongly recommend the work."

Spectator :—"Every one it may be presumed, has heard of Delmonico's the famous New York Restaurant ; a happy minority have been privileged to dine there."

Handy Volume Culinary Series. By Filippini
Oblong shape (6½ in. by 5in.), handsomely bound, 2s. 6d. each.

No. 1. ONE HUNDRED WAYS OF COOKING EGGS.

No. 2. ONE HUNDRED WAYS OF COOKING FISH.

No 3. ONE HUNDRED DESSERTS.

Queen :—" The publishers may be congratulated on the production of a set of books as valuable as they are dainty."

Mrs. RORER'S COOK BOOK. (Principal of the Philadelphia School
of Cookery). Crown 8vo., pp. 500, washable oil-cloth binding, 7s. 6d.

Queen :—"It may advisedly be asserted that this is a most valuable book and we know of few better calculated to take a front place in the book-shelf of a newly started housewife."

A GUIDE TO PALMISTRY. By Mrs. Eliza Easter Henderson.
24mo., illustrated, attractively bound, 2s. 6d.

Tablet :—" From the mere reading of this volume you can practise the art upon yourself, your friends, and the world at large."

Saturday Review :—"The book is simpler and easier read than the usual run of occult manuals. . . . The author professes to give the notes she has compiled for her own use."

WHEN CHARLES I. WAS KING. By J. S. Fletcher Popular

Edition. *Fifth.* Thick crown 8vo., cloth, artistic side design, 3s. 6d.

N.B. This novel has been styled the " Lorna Doone" of Yorkshire.

Spectator:—" It is quite worthy of a place beside the two romances— Walter Besant's "Dorothy Foster" and Conan Doyle's "Micah Clarke."

Graphic:—" An unusually successful attempt to realise unwritten history."

Daily News:—"Of hairbreadth escapes, of kidnappings, fightings, and stirring adventures, there are no end in the book. The account of the fight at Marston Moor is picturesquely and vigorously given. . . . . In this chronicle of the latter days of Charles I. there are many traces of studious rehearsals."

World:—" The battle narratives are well done, and there is a striking interview with Cromwell immediately after the execution of the King."

Vanity Fair :—''The incidents illustrate well the habits, ideas and state of the country in Charles I. reign. . . . . An excellent specimen of the historical novel."

Era :—" As a means of conveying a knowledge of history in an agreeable form to the rising generation. 'When Charles the First was King' may be specially recommended.''

Tablet :—" Mr. Fletcher's novel, of which a new and cheaper edition has been issued, may claim to rank among the best historical works."

Schoolmaster :—"The quarrels and battles of Roundheads and Cavaliers, the great fight at Marston Moor, the siege of Pontefract Castle, the Epoch-making trial of Charles I., and his death before the Banqueting Chamber in Whitehall are the background to this book. In the fore-ground one finds adventures galore, love-making, trials, narrow escapes, and all the stock-in-trade of the historical novelist. But there are simplicity and freshness, together with an artistic sense literature, in the book, redeeming it from the ordinary catalogue. is a book for elder boys and girls as well as adult readers."

Sheffield Telegraph:—" Hearty welcome is due to a new and popular edition of this admirable historical novel."

Daily Chronicle:—" The popular edition of this charming historical novel will undoubtedly prove one of the principal books of the season. . . . this work has undoubtedly raised the writer to foremost rank amongst the English novelists of the day. . . . . We cordially recommend it as a most appropriate and pleasing gift for the old, young, or middle-aged."

Leeds Mercury :—''As an historical romance, we have had nothing more worthy during recent years in fiction so treated—not even from Mr. Blackmore, or Mr. Besant, or Mr. Stevenson himself.''

PAVING THE WAY. A Romance of the Australian

Bush. By Simpson Newland, ex-Treasurer of South Australia. Popular Edition. Crown 8vo., cloth gilt, illustrated side, 3s. 6d.

** This volume is based upon exciting scenes and adventures which actually occurred in the pioneer days of Australia.

Daily Telegraph :—" It is a fine story, manifestly based on facts, and told with no less picturesqueness than vivacity. There is fighting enough in it, between 'black fellows' and 'white fellows,' bushrangers and mounted police, to satisfy the combative proclivities of the most sanguinary British Schoolboy."

Saturday Review :—" As can readily be imagined, any true description of life at such a time must abound in adventure, and in this respect Mr. Newland satisfies the cravings of the heartiest appetite. . . . Mr. Newland has found time to note the manners and customs of the black people (now fast dying out) and space to record some of their most curious legends."

Morning Post :—" Mr. Newland gives an account of Australian Pioneer life weaving truth and fiction with considerable ability. . . . 'Paving the Way' is no less to be commended as a romance of wild adventure, old with considerable spirit."

National Observer :—" It lifts the curtain from the squatter's life as few, if any recent books have done."

Publishers' Circular :—" Mr. Newland has written a romance not one whit inferior to those of Mr. Boldrewood."

South Australian Advertiser :—" Mr. Newland has produced a work which does very much for South Australia what 'Lorna Doone' has achieved for Devonshire. . . . It is evident to the reader that Mr. Newland's work is as truly a labour of love as was that of the Devonshire Novelist, and it is easy to predict for 'Paving the Way' a distinct place in colonial literature."

RUSSIAN RAMBLES. By Isabel F. Hapgood. Second Edition.

Crown 8vo., cloth, 6s. net.

CONTENTS :—I. Passports, Police, and Post-Office in Russia.—II. The Nevsky Prospekt.—III. My Experience with the Russian Censor —IV. Bargaining in Russia.—V. Experiences.—VI. A Russian Summer Resort.—VII. A Stroll in Moscow with Count Tolstoy.— VIII. Count Tolstoy at Home.—IX. A Russian Holy City.—X. A Journey on the Volga.—XI. The Russian Kumais Cure.—XII. Moscow Memories.—XIII. The Nizhni-Novgorod Fair and the Volga.

A WORKER IN IRON. A Fantasy. By Charles T. C. James,

Author of "On Turnham Green," "Yoke of Freedom," etc. Popular Edition. Crown 8vo., cloth, 2s. 6d.

Graphic:—"'A Worker in Iron' though called a fantasy, shows to great advantage over 'Miss Precocity' in the matter of truth to human nature and character."

Daily Chronicle:—"It is full of strong scenes and fine descriptions. Mr. James knows how to make an effective background, and his style is muscular, terse and picturesque."

Literary World:—"It is a purely romantic story. . . . . and the close of the story is most dramatic."

Northern Whig:—"Can be strongly recommended for a striking book, artistic in conception, and wrought out with no mean literary skill."

Realm:—"The plot is well worked out, and the giant smith, with the Titanic conflict of good and evil impulses raging in his heart, has a certain grandeur."

Western Mail:—"Still as the unattractive in nature is in Art often admired because of its skilful handling, there may be many readers who will find delight in the weird details of 'A Worker in Iron'."

ARTFUL ANTICKS. By Oliver Herford. Fcap. 4to., fully

illustrated, attractively bound in cloth, 6s.

*** A delightful holiday volume for the young, being a collection of humourous juvenile poems with clever illustrations on each page.

Queen:—"This is one of the most delightfully whimsical collections of sketches with both pen and pencil which are always so dear to the hearts of children. Mr. Herford's rhymes are full of that simple fun which it requires no effort to appreciate, and many of them are irresistibly ridiculous; while his graceful sketches show a high sense of genuine humour."

Graphic:—"Humorous books are scarce this season, but the few to hand are decidedly good. Such, for instance, as "Artful Anticks" by Oliver Herford, whose verses and pictures alike are full of genuine mirth and spirit."

Daily News—"Children will be pleased with 'Artful Anticks' by Oliver Herford, ... how delightful, for instance, is the little poem about the 'Geometrical Giraffe' and how true the truth it inculcates. . . . The sunny humour of this clever little volume and its hardly less clever illustrations, so thoroughly in keeping with its tone, will be highly appreciated by all who make its acquaintance."

Publishers' Circular:—"In the combination of his beautiful drawings with his verses, Mr. Herford has produced an entertaining and original book. . . . . It is among the most delightfully funny of the seasons' books."

A New Work on Evolution.

FALLEN ANGELS: A Disquisition upon Human Existence
—an Attempt to Elucidate some of its Mysteries, especially those of Evil and Suffering. By One of Them. Third and Popular Edition, revised and Index added, demy 8vo., cloth, 2s. 6d.

—————————Library Edition, cloth gilt, 6s.

This work has been the cause of much discussion and comment and many interesting letters have been received by the Author from Eminent Men in all branches of Thought.

Extract from a letter to the Author from the eminent Philologist, the Rev. Prof. W. W. SKEAT, *which is of considerable interest. May 30th,* 1894.—"I can well see that your book is the outcome of a good deal of long and patient thought. The subject is necessarily speculative, and incapable of exact proof; but it is very suggestive and interesting; and contains by the way, much that is curious and instructive. I am not myself gifted with any vividness of imagination, and am accustomed to deal only with the most obvious facts and experiences of daily life: nevertheless, I can appreciate much of it. And I may say that I am in full agreement with the general tone of the work, being naturally an 'optimist' of a most pronounced type, fully accepting the belief in continual progress and advancement. I must therefore heartily congratulate you on the completion of a work which is instinct with a spirit of trust and cheerfulness."

A very high dignitary of the Church of England writes as follows:—"I have been reading "Fallen Angels" with interest. Its tone of reverence and sympathy with all that is highest and best give great value to its suggestiveness."

From another eminent Authority in the Church:—"Your book treats a most interesting and a most mysterious subject, upon which, few even amongst theologians have bestowed anything like adequate attention. I have seen recently in German writers strong expressions of regret for the neglect to which it has been doomed."

A Peer, formerly a Minister of Her Majesty's Government, referring to "Fallen Angels" writes as follows:—"It is a time when we cannot afford to neglect any reasonable hypothesis or solution of the many pressing questions that are arising on all sides."

Popular Medical Monthly:—"This is a charming book."

Church Review:—"There is a good deal of curious learning in it, and many valuable quotations are given from mystical authors bearing on the subject. The advocate also pleads his difficult cause with eloquence and brilliancy. . . . Whatever we may think of its mysticism and bold theorising, the morality urged at the conclusion is good, and the final chapter 'Cui Bono?' one of the best of all."

Tablet:—"A thoughtful and very solemn attempt to solve the problem of human existence, and the mystery of good and evil."

Catholic Times:—"The style is bright, vigorous and clear, with an occasional spice of wit."

Critical Review:—"The extent to which literature, of all ages and departments, has been laid under requisition is most extraordinary."

Liverpoo Mercury:—"The book is written in a highly reverent and devotional spirit, and with an abundance of learning."

CONSTANTINOPLE. The City of the Sultans. By
C. E. Clement. Demy 8vo., with 20 Photogravures of Views and Objects
of Interest, handsomely bound in cloth, richly gilt, with cloth slip wrapper,
enclosed in cloth box, price 12s. 6d. net.

The Times—"'The City of the Sultans' is a pleasantly-written and well-illus-
trated account of Constantinople, its scenery and buildings, its history,
its antiquities, its institutions and its social life, by the lady who has
already treated Naples and Venice in a popular and attractive fashion."

The Publishers' Circular:—"One of the handsomest books of the year."

VENICE. The Queen of the Adriatic, or Venice, Mediæ-
val and Modern. By C. E. Clement. Demy 8vo. Twenty photogravures, bound uniformly with the above, 12s. 6d. net.

Scotsman:—"A beautiful book. . excellent reading. . sumptuously illustrated."

British Weekly:—"In typography, illustration, and binding, it is one of the
most sumptuous and tasteful books of the season. The illustrations
are quite faultless. . . . The letterpress is excellent."

NAPLES AND ITS ENVIRONS. By C. E. Clement. Demy
8vo., 20 photogravures bound uniformly with the above, 12s. 6d. net.

Times:—"Copiously and very attractively illustrated."

Glasgow Herald:—"Few cities have so picturesque a history as Naples. . . .
in her pages will be found most of the information which a general
reader can desire. . . . The Illustrations are beautiful, and there is a
good index."

FLORENCE. The Lily of the Arno, or Florence Past and
PRESENT. By Virginia W. Johnson. Demy 8vo., 25 Photogravures,
bound uniformly with the above, 12s. 6d. net.

Spectator.—"This handsome volume is a triumph—*it undoubtedly is a triumph*—
of illustration and typography, quite as much as of literature."

Queen:—"A sumptuous volume this. . . . . . It is enriched by photogravures
—really enriched, for most of these are admirable."

GENOA, THE SUPERB. The City of Columbus. By
Virginia W. Johnson. Demy 8vo., 20 photogravures bound uniformly
with the above, 12s. 6d. net.

Times:—"'Genoa the Superb' is a beautiful volume."

THE STORY OF A BAD BOY. By Thomas Bailey Aldrich.

Special Holiday Edition. With 9 Full-page and 56 Text Illustrations by A. B. Frost. Crown 8vo., tastefully bound in cloth gilt, 6s.

_{*} The American "Tom Brown's School Days," and the most popular boy's book in the United States.

Queen :—"Mr. Bailey Aldrich will fully maintain his reputation as an American humourist by this clever *jeu d'esprit.* The great charm of the book is its restrained humour. Never once does the author allow his sense of fun to run away with him, with the result that he has drawn a wonderfully realistic picture. It is impossible not to believe that one is reading the true and veracious story of the escapades of Tom Bailey, who is a regular pickle. But Mr. Bailey Aldrich is so very anxious to get 'extenuating circumstances' tacked on to the verdict, reiterating as he does that Tom was 'not such a bad boy after all,' that one is tempted to regard the book as in part at least autobiographical."

Saturday Review :—"This new edition of the best of American books for boys should rejoice the hearts of thousands of English boys, since it has in Mr. Frost a most able and sympathetic illustrator. You have only to open the book at hazard—here, let us say, at the scene of the mystic initiation of the 'Centipedes,' or at the drawing on the next page of the small boy-novice being 'gently checked' with the pitchfork—to be convinced that Mr. Frost is the artist elect to do justice to Mr. Aldrich's delightful book. There is no need to say more of a work that is surely, by now, an American classic. We are not surprised to learn that the author has received some two thousand letters asking him if his story is 'true.' We respect the tens of thousands of readers, young and old, who did not write, knowing the story to be true, as Scott, or as Shakespeare is true."

Realm :—"Mr. Aldrich's story might be described as the '*Tom Brown*' of America. It is full of bonfires, secret smoking parties, truancies, and hairbreadth escapes of all sorts, and these exciting materials lose nothing in Mr. A. B. Frost's illustrations. Especially thrilling is his weird illustration of the solemn ceremony of initiation into the mysterious order of the Centipedes. What boy can look at that and rest content till the book is his? No 'bad boy' could, at any rate: which is to say no boy worth his salt. For is it not the bad boys that make history? and Mr. Aldrich's purpose is the portrayal of a natural, healthy, good-hearted lad, 'blessed with fine digestive powers and no hypocrite'; one who is no cherub. Perhaps it is the boys who win the good-conduct prizes that are the really bad boys."

Sun :—"No more delightful book of its kind exists, and Mr. A. B. Frost has drawn a series of delicious pictures which will add new life to a lively friend."

Bookseller :—"Mr. A. B. Frost has enriched it with some sixty designs, which merit high praise for artistic perfection. . . . . In external form nothing better can be desired, the paper, print, and binding are alike admirable."

Publishers Circular :—"Mr. Aldrich is a consummate master of delicate and graceful prose, and he is at his best in the present story. . . . . In picturesqueness and imaginativeness it is not inferior to the best work of Bret Harte."

FAMOUS COMPOSERS AND THEIR WORKS. By Twenty-Six
Contributors, English, French, German and American, and profusely
illustrated. Edited by John Knowles Paine, Theodore Thomas and Karl
Klauser.

In four handsome quarto volumes, strongly bound in cloth, gilt side, price
Four Guineas Net. Detailed prospectus post free upon application.

The plan of this work is threefold:—First.—To give concise and authentic
biographies of the famous composers whose works are already familiar to
the world.—Second.—To give descriptions of the works of these composers
from which may be formed an intelligent estimate of their genius, their
influence on each other, and their position in musical history.—Third.—
To give a series of essays on the development and cultivation of the
principal forms of musical art in Italy, Germany, France, England,
America, and other countries.

The sixty-five biographies are fully illustrated by authentic portraits and
fine reproductions of photographs, engravings and paintings of historical
scenes relating to the personal history of each composer.

To obtain this collection the publishers sent a special representative for the
express purpose of searching the museums, public libraries and private
collections in Europe. The Cities of London, Paris, Berlin, Leipsic,
Vienna, Dresden, Florence and Rome have all contributed to this mass of
material which has never before been brought together.

Fac-similes of letters and manuscript music, views of birthplaces, residences,
monuments, medallions, statues, tombs, musical instruments, memorials,
and other rare and curious subjects, are here published for the first time,
and serve to bring into clear relief the personality and surroundings of
each composer.

This work is undoubtedly the finest work of its kind, the type, illustrations,
paper and binding being the best, and in addition to its being a handsome
table-book the following Eminent Musicians take great pleasure in
cordially recommending it to all Amateurs and Professionals, believing it
to be entitled to the highest consideration and support:—The late Sir
Joseph Barnby; Oscar Beringer, Esq.; Dr. J.F. Bridge; J.T. Carrodus, Esq.;
W. H. Cummings, Esq.; J. Spencer Curwen, Esq.; Edward Dannreuther,
Esq.; Sir George Grove; George Henschel, Esq.; Wm. Stevenson Hoyte,
Esq.; Sir A. C. Mackenzie; Dr. George C. Martin; E. Minshull, Esq.;
Dr. C. Hubert H. Parry; Ebenezer Prout, Esq.; Miss Ella Russell; Mons.
Emile Sauret; Mme. Lemmens Sherrington; John Thomas, Esq.;
Dr. E. H. Turpin; and many others.

EGYPT. Three Essays on the History, Religion, and
Art of Ancient Egypt. **By Martin Brimmer.** English edition
limited to 50 numbered copies. Royal 8vo., printed on hand-made
paper, and illustrated with 32 photogravures and a coloured map, handsomely bound in vellum, gilt, 30s. net. Three copies left.

SATCHEL GUIDE. For the Vacation Tourist in Europe.
The most popular Condensed European Guide published.
12mo., maps, limp leather, 6s. net.

ADAMS CABLE CODEX. Paper 1s. Net, cloth 2s. Net.

This little Code covers every possible contingency, whether it be pleasure or
business, and once tried will always be recommended.

SCANDINAVIAN AND RUSS or, by Way of the Baltic.
By John Albert Manton, M.R.C.S., Eng., L.R.C.P., Lond., etc.
Being an account of the Cruise of the Steam Yacht "St.
Sunniva" to the Northern Capitals. May—June, 1895. Crown,
8vo. Profusely Illustrated with Maps, Photographs (taken *en route*),
Portraits, Sketches and Facetiae. Sewed 2s.

THE INDEX GUIDE TO TRAVEL AND ART STUDY IN
EUROPE. **By L. C. Loomis.** New and Enlarged Edition. 12mo.,
leather, 15s.

. This Work is an Index to everything worth seeing in Europe. Besides
containing Plans, Maps, and 160 Illustrations of Pictures in the best Galleries, it
contains Catalogues of the Chief Collections, and every information useful to the
Tourist.

THE BORDERLAND OF CZAR AND KAISER. Notes from both
sides of the Russian Frontier. **By Poultney Bigelow.** Crown 8vo., 60
charming illustrations, being reproductions of drawings and photographs
taken on the spot by F. Remington, tastefully bound, 7s. 6d. net.

Times.—"Lively sketches, military, social and political, . . . shrewd and
well-informed and very skilfully illustrated."

Field.—"We cannot conclude this [long] notice without a word of praise for
the excellent illustrations by Mr. Remington. They add considerably
to the value of the book."

Pall Mall Gazette.—"His book is always the pleasantest possible reading."

Graphic.—"And when the great war does come, Mr. Bigelow's fascinating book
will be of the greatest value to all students of the game."

LLANARTRO: A Welsh Idyll. By Mrs. Fred Reynolds'

Popular Edition. Crown 8vo., cloth, 3s. 6d.

Athenæum.—"The author distinguishes with considerable subtlety between the feelings of *camaraderie* that Inez has for the earlier aspirant Hugh, and the tumultuous and disquieting passion inspired by the more romantic Lawrence; and the way in which the friendship of the two men is undiminished in spite of all is finely told. The charm of the story is enhanced by its setting in the Snowdon district of Wales."

Yorkshire Post.—"Where a writer of the modern school would have shown us only the workings of the worst of passions, Mrs. Reynolds has drawn a picture of self-sacrifice which can only be helpful to the reader. Such books are all too few; but the charm of "Llanartro" is so complete that it may do the work of many less successful efforts."

British Weekly.—"There is great beauty and tenderness in Mrs. Reynolds idyll. Two college friends who adore one another fall in love with the same girl. Happily she has no doubt in her own mind which she loves, although she likes both. Mrs. Reynolds, instead of working out this situation to a development of jealousy, hatred, treachery, and blood, brings out of it manly fidelity and noble sacrifice. The delicacy with which the characters are elaborated is matched by the exquisite skill with which Mrs. Reynolds gives her readers all the enjoyment of breathing fresh country air and living amid lovely Welsh landscape. Mrs. Reynolds is a true artist, and this specimen of her work is sure to win many readers. All will admit that it is a true idyll."

Sheffield Telegraph.—"The story is well put together, the scenery is pretty, and the sentiment and characters are altogether charming."

Methodist Recorder.—"Answers absolutely to its designation. It is a pure prose poem—a glorification of self-sacrifice. With a true artist's skill Mrs. Reynolds outlines for us three or four delightful characters, each full of individuality. There is not a disagreeable sentence in the book, and its tone is as elevating as its literary value is high."

Scotsman.—"A pretty and well-written love story. The story is a work of much merit."

Dr. GRAY'S QUEST. By Francis H. Underwood, LL.D.

(late U.S. Consul at Edinburgh). Crown 8vo., cloth gilt, 6s.

Glasgow Herald.—"Charmingly written . . . an excellent story."

Scotsman.—"Will be found to give genuine pleasure and insight. Keen observation and penetrating sympathy are in them, and certain of the persons, in this drama—as, for example, Mercy Starkweather—exhibit a marked creative power. She is not like any other character in fiction, and yet she is true to nature. She is at once hateful and attractive. James Gray is set over against her by way of contrast—the idealist's as against the sensualist's conception of life and its duties. . . . other characters are drawn with humour and intimate knowledge; and there are scenes in the story—for instance, that between Mrs. Kenmore and Winterton—that linger long in the reader's memory."

World.—"The late Dr. Underwood, whose last work 'Dr. Gray's Quest' was a writer to whom the obsolete epithet 'elegant' distinctly applies. When, as in his case, there is no weakness about the elegance, the latter is charming. The story of the Quest undertaken by a young doctor with the object of proving the innocence of a convict under sentence of long imprisonment for a daring forgery, is singularly touching, and has several side-issues. The story is not a cheerful one even at the end, although Dr. Gray is successful in his quest, but it is convincingly true."

North British Daily Mail.—"It is impossible to deny the charm with which the whole of this pathetic story is permeated; we feel it in the hold the various characters have of our sympathies, and though the work may fall short of being a notable novel, yet the late Dr. Underwood had to an uncommon degree the power of making all his characters live—they are real entities to the reader."

Methodist Times.—"An admirable story."

Daily Chronicle :—"Mr. Underwood knows womankind, and his skill in characterisation is very considerable. His creations stand out distinct, unique. The admirable way in which he has sketched the New England life of forty years ago, shows that he must have written from actual experience and quick observation. His story is interesting and probable, without troubling us with petty and sordid details, he, by clever suggestion, compels us to realise much of life's seamy side. In his style there is an old-fashioned precision and a somewhat didactic flavour, but his English is excellent, and he has a due sense of the importance of words and phrases. As a whole, the book is a thorough and an artistic piece of work."

TWO YEARS ON THE ALABAMA. By Lieut. Arthur
Sinclair, C.S.N. Royal 8vo., 32 illustrations, cloth gilt, 15s.

This is a faithful and first account of the life and experiences on board the "Alabama," from its inception to its foundering, written by Lieut. Sinclair, one of its officers.

The Times :—" Recent events and the anxieties from which the country is even now not altogether free, give a certain opportuneness to the publication of Lieutenant Arthur Sinclair's book, 'Two Years on the Alabama.' The official record of the career of that very expensive vessel was long ago written by its commander, Captain Semmes ; but that, as the author of the present volume remarks, ' was most carefully confined within the limits of legal and professional statement. It was no part of Captain Semmes' purpose to enter into the details of life on board or to make any unnecessary confidences respecting himself or the officers and crew who shared his labours and successes.' To the official story Lieutenant Sinclair here adds a lively and most readable supplement, based apparently on diaries written at the time, and giving us those very details of daily existence, from the moment when the Alabama stole out of Liverpool to the moment when the Kearsarge sent her to the bottom, which the unofficial reader asks for in naval history. The whole amazing story is told in a very vivid way, and Lieutenant Sinclair writes of his ship, his captain, and his crew with the enthusiasm which is natural to a spirited naval officer. . . Of the greater incidents, the chief are the combat in the Gulf of Mexico with the United States ship Hatteras, which was sunk by the Alabama after a fight of thirteen minutes—' probably the quickest naval duel on record' —and the only other fight experienced by the Alabama, her disastrous engagement with the Kearsarge. The whole story of this, beginning with the formal challenge sent by Semmes to his enemy in Cherbourg Harbour and ending with the rescue of the swimming survivors by the English yacht Deerhound, is told in a very lively and picturesque fashion by Lieutenant Sinclair."

Daily Telegraph :—" Whatever the reason for the delay, we may be glad that the author has, even at the eleventh hour, rescued from oblivion so many interesting incidents connected with the famous cruiser, and given us both photographic and literary portraits of all the officers on board. . . . . The engagement with the Hatteras is an exciting episode, and there are enough fights and adventures in the book to satisfy the most exacting."

Daily News :—" The Alabama. the most famous cruiser in naval history, was commissioned on the 24th August, 1862. She fought her last fight off Cherbourg on Sunday, the 19th June, 1864. Men, only now middle-aged, can remember, almost as if it were yesterday, the excitement which this fight excited all over Europe."

Daily Chronicle :—" Mr. Sinclair has given us a book whose pages must be consulted by any historian of the Civil War, while it is fairly readable by the generation of to-day which has grown up since the duel in the Channel two and thirty years ago."

STORIES OF NORWAY in the Saga Days. By Mary Howarth. Imperial 16mo., illustrated with four charming drawings by F. Hamilton Jackson, attractively bound, 3s. 6d.

Bazaar :—" ' Stories of Norway in the Saga Days' might have been written by Mr. William Morris, whose thoughts when not absorbed by social matters invariably fly Volsung and Viking-ward. Miss Mary Howarth gives us four stories taken from old Norse sources, and clothed in English prose; well clothed too, for she has managed to make them as interesting as an Eastern fairy tale. . . . This is a book that can be bought to give away with a feeling of satisfaction that it is worth its cost."

North British Daily Mail :—" These are delightfully-written stories of Old Norway, when the saga was the literary expression of a romantic and superstitious people, delightful in their quaint old-worldliness of style and thought, their child-like openness, and their confidence in the native joyousness of human nature. . . . Full of tender pathos and innocent mirth."

Daily Chronicle :—" Smoothly and pleasantly told. . . . The book ought to find much favour about Christmas time."

Glasgow Herald :—"Very gracefully told, and the book will be a pleasant present for thoughtful young people."

Daily Graphic :—" ' Stories of Norway in the Saga Days' by Mary Howarth, well illustrated by F. Hamilton Jackson will interest many children in the old Scandinavian legends which, familiar though they may be to many of us, have never been popularised among the younger generation."

Scotsman :—" Four spirited tales founded on the ancient heroic history of Scandinavia, and told in a pleasant manner. . . The tales are well illustrated."

Globe :—"Told in a way which is sure to catch the attention of the elder nursery folk ; and illustrated nicely."

Vanity Fair :—" We have read nothing else that so nearly approaches 'Tales from Iceland' in quiet excellence as Mrs. Howarth's 'Stories of Norway' . . here is a book that mothers should be glad to give to their children who can read, or to read to those who cannot."

Literary World :—"Four well-sustained stories hold the reader's attention from cover to cover."

To-Day :—"All young people will delight in this book, and some older ones, too."

Princess :—" A delightful book for young folks. . . . Full of romance and mysticism of the North. . . . All the stories are of a really fascinating character, and very quaintly and prettily related."

Lady's Pictorial :—"The ever-popular Scandinavian stories lose none of their charm in the hands of Mary Howarth, for this collection is exceedingly attractive. The illustrations add not a little to the charm of the book."

Home Chat :—"Forms a delightful volume, and as a Christmas present it would be hard to beat."

THE SONG OF HIAWATHA. By Henry Wadsworth

Longfellow. Post 8vo., with a new etched portrait and 22 full-page illustrations by Frederic Remington, tastefully bound in cloth, gilt top, 7s. 6d. net.

The demand for an artistic but inexpensive edition of this unique poem has led the publishers to bring it out in a new and very attractive form. It has been carefully printed, with 22 full-page illustrations by Frederic Remington, whose pictures of Indians and Indian life are not drawn from fancy but from years of study on the plains of the West. The book has an etched portrait of Mr. Longfellow, which is regarded as one of the best ever made of him, and which shows how he looked at the time "Hiawatha" was written.

> *Glasgow Herald* :—"A charming Christmas book. . . . The special attractiveness of this edition lying in the beautiful illustrations. They number over a score, and in all of them Mr. Frederic Remington has shown a remarkable appreciation of the spirit of the poem, nor are technical skill and delicacy of finish less conspicuous in the reproduction of them. The forest scenes, with their play of light and shade, afforded opportunities of which advantage has been taken by the artist to produce the most effective contrasts and gradations of tone; and the closest and most critical examination only serves to justify, and, indeed, to increase, the admiration which the most cursory inspection cannot fail to excite."

> *Scotsman* :—"It is printed in the beautiful type of the Riverside Press. . . The poem is introduced by a readable and brief note by an unnamed writer, and graced by a series of charming illustrations from designs by Mr. Frederic Remington. The pictures succeed in catching the spirit of the poem as an epic of the noble red man, and make this edition a particularly desirable one."

> *Publishers' Circular* :—"The illustrations are indeed beyond all praise, each one is a finished picture."

CHILDHOOD IN LITERATURE AND ART; with some Observations on Literature for Children. A Study by Horace E. Scudder. Crown 8vo., cloth, 5s. net.

FRAIL CHILDREN OF THE AIR. Excursions into the World of Butterflies. Containing 9 full-page Illustrations. By Samuel Hubbard Scudder. Crown 8vo., cloth, 6s. net.

ABOUT PARIS. By Richard Harding Davis. Profusely Illustrated by CHARLES DANA GIBSON. Crown 8vo., cloth, 6s. 6d.

PUSHING TO THE FRONT: or Success under Difficulties.

A book of inspiration and encouragement to all who are struggling for self-elevation along the paths of knowledge and of duty. By **Orison Swett Marden**, *Author of "Architects of Fate."* Crown 8vo., 24 portraits, cloth, gilt top, 6s. net.

Daily Chronicle:—"The book is thoroughly readable, for Mr. Marden has spared no pains to bring together an immense number of attractive anecdotes and quotations."

Schoolmaster:—"Mr. Marden may be congratulated on having produced a volume so exceptionally well-written and interesting, that we do not doubt it will take high rank among the best books that have been brought out as a stimulus and encouragement to aspiring youth. Indeed, since the appearance of Dr. Smiles' "Self Help," we do not remember having seen anything so admirable in literary style and high purpose as Mr. Marden's 'Pushing to the Front.' The design of the book is to influence, less by argument and appeal, than by stirring example and incident, and the four hundred pages are crowded with brightly told information concerning the great efforts of noble men and women, who have won success in spite of overwhelming difficulties."

The author tells us in his preface that he devoted all his spare moments for ten years to the work when a fire destroyed the whole of his manuscripts and notes, and he had to begin again. His own life is, therefore, in keeping with the purpose of his admirable volume, and lends to it the additional interest attaching to the words of one who can practice as well as preach. The book is illustrated with twenty-four very good full-page portraits of men and women who have struggled and succeeded, among the best being those of Bismarck, Gladstone, Franklin, James Watt, Oliver Wendell Holmes, and Darwin."

A HARMONY OF THE GOSPELS FOR HISTORICAL STUDY.

An Analytical Synopsis of the Four Gospels in the Version o 1881. By **William Arnold Stevens** and **Ernest De Witt Burton**. Small 4to. cloth, 7s. 6d.

British Weekly:—"This is a scholarly and useful harmony, and ought to be in the hands of serious students. . . . The notes are careful and not too numerous, and altogether we do not know a better work of the kind."

Christian World:—"The work has many special points, and will be of great value to students."

Methodist Times:—"The careful reader of the New Testament will rejoice in such an accessory to his Biblical apparatus.

ROOKS AND THEIR NEIGHBOURS. By J. G. Sowerby.
Super royal 8vo., 34 illustrations by the author, cloth, 6s. net.

The Times :—"' Rooks and their Neighbours' is a prettily-illustrated volume of pleasant gossip about Rooks by a writer who, while making no pretence to be scientific, has kept his eyes open, and has observed with care and sympathy the manners and customs of his rookery."

Land and Water :—"Mr. Sowerby is obviously a careful and patient observer, and has a pleasantly humorous way of recording his impressions."

The Scotsman :—"Mr. Sowerby knows his rooks. He has watched them day and night, and summer and winter. . . . The volume will yield, along with much amusement, not a little information. It is seasoned throughout, and with good taste, with the author's pleasant wit."

MODERN MECHANISM. Exhibiting the latest Progress in
Machines, Motors, and the Transmission of Power. Edited by **Park Benjamin, LL.B., Ph.D.,** *Editor of "Appletons' Cyclopædia of Applied Mechanics."* Royal 8vo., pp. 926, 50 full-page plates and about 1500 cuts, cloth extra, 15s. net.

Nature :—"It is only just to congratulate the editor on the completion of a work which must prove useful to many, and which should find a place in all technical libraries."

Electricity :—"The articles are quite up to date, and fully illustrated, and we think the book should prove useful to a large circle of readers. We would especially commend the portions devoted to dynamos, motors and the electrical transmission of power."

Engineer :—"As a record of what has been done, and a careful digest of all the more important considerations which underlie, or principles which have guided these modern accomplishments, this will be found a valuable book of reference."

Machinery :—"A more admirably compiled or more carefully edited publication than 'Modern Mechanism' has not been issued within our recollection."

Electrical Review :—"One of the most important and useful of its kind hitherto published. . . . Taking the work altogether, it would be difficult to praise it too highly; it should prove a marked success."

KENNEL SECRETS. How to Breed, Exhibit, and Manage
Dogs. By "Ashmont." One Volume 4to., pp. 362, 28 portraits of owners, 145 portraits of celebrated dogs. Beautifully printed on plate paper and handsomely bound, price 16s. net.

THE RULERS OF THE MEDITERRANEAN. By Richard
Harding Davis, Author of "Gallegher," "Van Bibber," &c. Crown
8vo., 53 charming illustrations, cloth gilt, 6s.

Globe:—"A book of travel of more than ordinary interest and value."

Daily News:—"He is a lively, gossiping companion, and his observations and
experiences are full of entertaining glimpses of Oriental life."

Glasgow Herald:—"Vivacious and pleasant reading."

Bookman:—"Mr. Harding Davis is a charming writer, and in describing even
hackneyed places and things he is very readable. These papers on
Gibraltar, Tangier, Cairo, Athens, and Constantinople are pleasanter
than most travel records. English readers will find the chapter on
"The Englishman in Egypt" of special interest to them, and the
judgment of an impartial American is not to be dismissed as valueless."

THROUGH STARLIGHT TO DAWN. By A. Ernest
Hinshelwood. Second Edition. Crown 8vo., printed on hand-made paper
at the Chiswick Press, tastefully bound, 5s. net

Scotsman:—"Though they are by no means an imitation, these poems have
much in common with the work of Mr. Swinburne. . . . They reveal
a power which promises better things."

Manchester Examiner:—"Besides the striking originality and suggestiveness
of his verses, they are remarkably rhythmical. They have the true
poetic ring, and show that he has great command over metre."

THE AMERICAN SIBERIA: or, Fourteen Years' Expe-
rience in a Southern Convict Camp. By J. C. Powell. Crown
8vo., illustrated, cloth, 3s. 6d.

Daily Telegraph:—"Decidedly interesting. . . Many exciting pages."

Spectator:—"His experiences are full of interesting and often fascinating
incidents."

Manchester Courier:—"A strong and engrossing story."

ALDRICH'S POEMS. A New and Complete Library Edition.
Demy 8vo., fine engraved portrait and illustrations, cloth extra, 6s.

To-Day —"The most attractive of living American Poets."

LOVE LYRICS. By Alan Stanley. Fcap, 8vo., cloth, 2s. 6d. nett.

Academy:—"Mr. Stanley manages some difficult metres very deftly, he
expresses his thoughts felicitously, and shows genuine poetical feeling."

THE ART OF TAKING A WIFE. By Paolo Mantegazzi.
Third Edition.   Fcap 8vo., neatly bound, 3s. 6d.

CONTENTS :—Prologue.—I. Marriage in Modern Society.—II. Sexual
Choice in Marriage—The art of choosing well.—III. Age and
Health.—IV. Physical Sympathy—Race and Nationality.—V. The
Harmony of Feelings.—VI. Harmony of Thoughts.—VII. The
Financial Question in Marriage.—VIII. The Incidents and Acci-
dents of Marriage.—IX. Hell.—X. Purgatory.—XI. Paradise.

Sun :—"The whole work is alive with literary taste, and the English publishers
are to be sincerely congratulated and thanked for introducing so
healthy an exposition to English readers.   It cannot be questioned
that the number of those readers will be legion."

Yorkshire Post:—"Deals boldly with the dark side of married life. . . The
volume is very tastefully got up, and deserves to be widely read, but,
as we have said, it is not a book for young people."

SUNSET PASS: or, Running the Gauntlet Through
Apache Land.   By Captain Charles King.   Illustrated.   Author
of "The Deserter," "A War-time Wooing."   Crown 8vo., cloth, 3s. 6d.

Athenæum :—"A well-told story of adventure, with all the freshness of
American wild life in the West."
Review of Reviews :—"Sensational and pleasing enough in all conscience."
Scottish Leader :—"The tale is one of thrilling interest, and once begun there is
no laying it down till the last page is reached."

A QUESTION OF TIME. By Gertrude Franklin Atherton,
Author of "The Doomswoman," "Hermia Suydam," "Los Cerritos,"
etc., etc.   Crown 8vo., Cloth, 3s. 6d.

Athenæum :—"Shows distinct power. . . . . . The hero and heroine win the
reader's sympathies almost from the first, while the scandal they
create in the prim New England town of Dunforth is effectively
sketched."
Scottish Leader :—"As novel in conception as it is admirable in execution."

MARIONETTES. By Julien Gordon, Author of "A Diplomat's
Diary," "Puritan Pagan," &c.   Crown 8vo., cloth, 3s. 6d.

Athenæum:—"The book is so excellent . . . . . The minor Characters are
admirably done. . . . . . The dramatic abruptness and clearness are
beyond praise."
Scottish Leader:—"The character sketching is exquisite, and the style is brilliant. . . . A novel of remarkable power and brilliancy."

THE DARLEYS OF DINGO DINGO. By J. C. MacCartie.

Popular Edition. Crown 8vo., attractively bound, 3s. 6d.

A story of Modern Australian Country Life.

Manchester Courier.—"We must thank the writer for giving us something really fresh and new, a bright, vigorous, wholesome study of Australian life, with a healthy, open-air, breezy tone about it all which refreshes like a sea-bath . . . always interesting, and we learn a good deal of valuable information about colonial life."

Daily Telegraph.—"To the above names (Mrs. Campbell Praed, Rolf Boldrewood, and E. W. Hornung) as associated with vivid and fascinating description of latter-day life in Australia, must now be added that of J. C. MacCartie, whose novel "The Darleys of Dingo Dingo," is simply delightful reading throughout."

Athenæum.—"Many of the characters introduced are cleverly drawn."

Spectator.—"The book is very enjoyable and Australian, and thoroughly wholesome."

Manchester Guardian.—"Mr. MacCartie can hit off oddities of character with a good deal of humour."

Glasgow Herald.—" Good humour reigns supreme throughout this book ."

IESÄT NASSAR. The Story of the Life of Jesus the Nazarene. By Peter Amra and B. A. F. Mamreoy. Thick 8vo., 712 pp., cloth, 10s.

The Standard says :—"This volume is suited to those desirous of gathering all the information obtainable upon the most important of all subjects, and capable of weighing the matter placed before them. It is the work of persons having exceptional advantages and opportunities for research, and for the attainment of information on matters social and religious, in Syria, Palestine, and in Egypt, where they had resided for many years. They were born in Jerusalem of Russian parents, who took up their residence in the Holy Land with the object for seeking knowledge that would cast a light upon the conflicting dogmas and doctrines of the Christian, Jewish, and Mohammedan creeds, obtaining for the purpose a special Firman from the Sultan, which placed them in communication with ruling Mohammedan families. The story of the life of Jesus here given is founded on Christian and Jewish Secular and Ecclesiastical Histories, and on Traditions and Legends of Oriental and Occidental Nations. . . . No one can lay down the book without feeling that he has acquired much knowledge of the circumstances and events among which His life was carried out, and of the various accounts that have been preserved of Him, gathered from a great variety of sources."

NO HEROES. By Blanche Willis Howard. Author of
"A Battle and a Boy," "Guenn," "One Summer," etc., etc. Imperial
16mo., illustrated, cloth extra, 2s. 6d.

Speaker :—"There is a certain artless simplicity, as well as real ability about
'No Heroes '—a story of the pluck and indeed, unselfish devotion of a
New England lad."

Publishers' Circular :—"Rarely indeed is it that children's stories fall into the
reviewer's hands so marked with freshness, liveliness, humour,
pathos, and clever character-drawing."

THE WITCH OF THE JUNIPER WALK, and other Fairy
Tales. By Mrs. Frank May. Impl. 16mo., 17 Illustrations by the
Author, handsomely bound in bevelled cloth, with attractive side design,
2s. 6d.

Times :—"They are highly romantic."

JACK'S PARTNER, and other Stories. By Stephen Fiske.
With Introduction by JOSEPH HATTON. Crown 8vo., bevelled cloth, gilt
top, 2s. 6d.

Athenæum :—"Mr. Joseph Hatton's brief introductory account of the author
suggests the idea that in Mr. Fiske we have the George Sims
of America, a suggestion which is confirmed by a perusal of his book."

World :—"Vivid, graphic, and humourous. . . . They are all clever."

Pall Mall Gazette :—"A collection of pretty bright stories."

Scotsman :—"Admirably told."

THOUGHTS OF BUSY GIRLS. Written by a group of girls
who have little time for study, and yet who find much time for
thinking. Edited by Grace H. Dodge. 24mo., bevelled cloth, 1s. 6d.

HELEN BRENT, M.D. A Social Study. 24mo., bevelled
cloth, 1s. 6d.

Literary World :—"This is a study of American life, in which the author with
the courage bred by Ibsenism, attacks a great social evil. . . . It is
delicately and well handled."

HYMNS FOR PRIVATE USE. Collected by Rev. H. C.
Shuttleworth, Vicar of St. Nicholas Cole-Abbey. 32mo., cloth,
1s. net

THE PRESIDENTS OF THE UNITED STATES, 1789-1894.

Written by John Fiske, Carl Schurz, William E. Russell, Daniel C. Gilman, William Walter Phelps, Robert C. Winthrop, George Bancroft, John Hay, and others. Edited by John James Wilson. Large 8vo. Illustrated with 23 beautiful steel engravings and over 100 facsimiles of autograph letters, portraits and views in the text. Cloth, gilt top, 12s. 6d. net.

Times.—"An English reader who is provided with this book and Mr. Goldwin Smith's 'Political Sketch' together with a good series of historical maps, will hardly want more to enable him to understand in outline the history of the United States."

THE STORY OF THE ATLANTIC TELEGRAPH. By Henry

M. Field. Crown 8vo., pp. 426, portrait and woodcuts, cloth, gilt top, 7s. 6d.

Times:—"THE STORY OF THE ATLANTIC TELEGRAPH, by Henry M. Field is at once the record of one of the greatest of modern international enterprises and the associated biography of the man whose name it should render immortal."

SIR FRANCIS BACON'S CIPHER STORY. Discovered and

Deciphered. By Orville W. Owen, M.D. Vols. I. and II. out. Royal 8vo., cloth, 10s. 6d. net. each.

REFLECTIONS OF A "WALL-FLOWER." By "Laura

Washington." Small 4to., printed on hand-made paper, sewed, 1s.

CONTENTS.—Introductory—Explanatory—On Gentlemen—Jealousy—Humility—On Ancestry—Mother's Music—On Bores—Conversation—On Politeness, or Chinese Parties—Partners I have had —On Love Making—Final.

Scotsman.—"Will be read with interest."

Manchester Guardian.—"These 'Reflections' are more restful than Problem Novels."

THE BUILDERS OF AMERICAN LITERATURE. Being

Biographical Sketches of American Authors born previous to 1826. By F. H. Underwood. *First Series.* Crown 8vo., cloth, gilt top, 7s. 6d.

Sun :—"Of great value to the English reader and the English journalist."

THE JEWISH QUESTION and THE MISSION OF THE JEWS.
Crown 8vo., pp. 340, cloth, gilt top, 7s. 6d.

Times:—"His book is at once an historical defence of the Jews and the part that they have played in European civilization."

Jewish Chronicle:—"As Jews, we must be grateful to the author for his sympathetic tone, his brave attacks on anti-Semitism, and for the industry and perseverance with which he has worked out his subject."

Morning Post:—"A powerful vindication of the Jewish race."

SPERRY STORIES. 24mo., paper wrapper, 1s.

A collection of short stories which appeared in "The Idler," "To-Day," etc.

ZADOC PINE AND OTHER STORIES. By H. C. Bunner.
Editor of New York "Puck." Crown 8vo., cloth gilt, 5s.

Morning Post:—"By turns pathetic, keenly observant, and tenderly imaginative. Mr. Bunner is proficient in the art of writing short stories."

A DOUBLE LIFE. By Ella Wheeler Wilcox. Author of
"Poems of Passion" and "Poems of Pleasure," etc. Crown 8vo., cloth, 2s.

Glasgow Herald:—"A short story of excellent moral. . . . . The characters are strongly drawn, and most of them are decidedly interesting."

A HISTORY OF PERU. By Clements R. Markham.
Demy 8vo., 25 full-page illustrations and 5 maps, cloth gilt, 10s. 6d.

Athenæum:—"Few people possess better qualifications than Mr. Markham for writing a History of Peru. . . . . We congratulate Mr. Markham upon his excellent Sketches of the better class of society in Peru, its scenery and its antiquities. There is a swing and a dash about his style which impresses the reader and bears him irresistably along."

A HISTORY OF CHILI. By Anson Uriel Hancock. Demy
8vo., 9 illustrations and 3 maps, cloth gilt, 10s. 6d.

Saturday Review:—"Mr. Hancock claims to have given for the first time in English a complete account of Chili. . . . . We may congratulate him on having achieved his design. . . . Mr. Hancock's virtues are those of the painstaking chronicler. And he has those virtues in full quantity."

South American Journal:—"We have nothing but commendation for Mr. Hancock's 'History of Chili.' . . The story is brought down to the end of 1892."

www.ingramcontent.com/pod-product-compliance
Lightning Source LLC
Chambersburg PA
CBHW031334070726
47496CB00018B/1853